UNMARKED

Kate Hansen

First Published in Australia by Aurora House
www.aurorahouse.com.au

This edition published 2018
Copyright @ Kate Hansen 2018
Typesetting: Allen Smalley
Cover design: Simon Critchell

ISBN number: 978-0-6483508-7-3 (paperback)

National Library of Australia Cataloguing in Publication entry:

 NATIONAL LIBRARY OF AUSTRALIA

A catalogue record for this book is available from the National Library of Australia

Distributed by:
Ingram Content:
https://www.ingramcontent.com/
Australia: phone +613 9765 4800 | email lsiaustralia@ingramcontent.com
Milton Keynes UK: phone +44 (0)845 121 4567 | email enquiries@ingramcontent.com
La Vergne, TN USA: phone 1-800-509-4156 | email inquiry@lightningsource.com

Gardners UK:
https://www.gardners.com/
phone +44 (0)1323 521555 | email: sales@gardners.com

Bertrams UK:
https://www.bertrams.com/BertWeb/index.jsp
phone +44 (0)1603 648400 | email sales@bertrams.com

000-01-000

I HAD PASSED THEM many times before without paying attention, but this time, driving along the same stretch of asphalt as I did everyday, I noticed a small group of shops. Three of the shop fronts appeared freshly painted, but with the surrounding stores looking like they should be condemned, it seemed their owners' efforts had been pointless. And yet, they actually had a few patrons and several well-dressed young customers walking the cracked footpath and entering through their doorways.

The street itself wasn't unpleasant; there were just none of the exciting multinational franchises I was used to. You drove past (or at least I did) because you knew you could purchase your stuff much more cheaply at a big supermarket. This time though I was really thirsty so I was going to have to stop and pay those few extra cents. My fear of being taken advantage of was fading fast.

It was the first time I had actually noticed other shoppers here. I now found myself a little excited, as I'd heard that these shops sold their soft drinks cold, a huge improvement on the warm rubbish I was used to buying.

As I strolled past the fruit shop, I was so overcome with the fresh smell I felt a strange urge to eat fruit. Of course I ignored it and continued on. Then the aroma of coffee and pastry filled the air and my desire for a soft drink was quickly replaced. Ahead I could see the source – a well-patronised coffee shop, flowing out onto the footpath, with people smiling, laughing and obviously enjoying the great food. Now I was annoyed I didn't have the time to stop and eat, but it didn't matter. I decided this was to be my new spot to shop and drink coffee with my friends. I would become the trendsetter of my group, instead of my usual role as the happy follower.

Impressed by my new resolve, I entered the slightly run-down general store confidently as if I were already a regular patron. I stared into the drink fridge pretending to consider a bottle of water (I wasn't really!)but quickly grabbed a sugary soda. At only twenty-six, I had plenty of time to become health conscious later. I could hear the only other customer chatting away to the sweet-looking, elderly male shopkeeper. They knew each other's names with no name tag to be seen. I found this quite exciting. I could just imagine shopping on this stretch and, in time, "How are you going today, Elisha?" I could really get used to that. It certainly beat "Number 25" when I picked up the lunches at work. The same shop five days a week and that's what I got.

I began daydreaming of shopping here in the future. After a long day answering the phone to people who didn't want to talk to me anyway, I could drop in here on my way home and chat to the shopkeepers, telling them about my day at work. They might at least pretend to care, unlike my friends who just wanted to talk about their wonderful boyfriends, who weren't always that wonderful.

I rested my can on the counter and added a chocolate bar that had been strategically placed in the line of sight for those of us with no self-control. It is a very clever shop man oeuvre but one that I'm a big fan of – nothing worse than realising you felt like a chocolate when you've already left the shop.

"Good morning," said the man behind the counter, with a smile, "Beautiful day out there." I smiled and agreed while I handed him my card, which he politely declined. He explained to me that they didn't take cards for purchases under twenty dollars. Well, I did not take that well at all, and I started abusing the poor man like a spoilt two year old. I pointed out that nobody carried cash anymore and that he was a stupid old fool who was not going to be in business much longer. I didn't see his reaction as I stormed out of the shop empty-handed but I assume he was a little stunned. He should have given me the middle-finger salute I deserved but he was so nice I doubt that he did.

Heading towards my pitiful excuse for a car, I continued mumbling abuse at the shopping strip with probably more volume than was necessary. "Backward, small-town losers! You'll be wiped out by multinationals soon enough and I can't wait."

In my fit of rage I fumbled around in my bag trying to find my car keys, which I promptly dropped on the ground, and then banged my head hard on the side rear-vision mirror, causing an almighty bang and drawing unwanted attention from a man I could only hope hadn't heard my rant. To be honest there was no way he could have missed it but, like a true gentleman, he just calmly asked if I was alright. To make matters worse, he wasn't just a man. He was ridiculously gorgeous, possibly the most perfect specimen I had ever seen. Embarrassed beyond words, I said I was fine and jumped into my car faster than if I were in danger.

I slumped into my seat and from the illusory safety of my car watched the man of my dreams walk away, before I spotted a twenty dollar note in my console. I had cash! Enough for a drink, chocolate and a box of aspirin to help ease the pain of the now-throbbing bump on my head, but after my behaviour, I wasn't going back into that shop. A better person would have marched back, apologised profusely, bought what they needed and left a big tip, hoping Prince Charming was there to notice this strong, confident woman and ask her out.

Unfortunately that person wasn't me. Courage was something I'd thought I had while I was abusing an innocent old man, but that was just obnoxious behaviour. True courage I didn't have, and now I was destined to a lonely, thirsty future. I'd probably find another drink but would another man ever come close to the now-blown-completely-out-of-proportion, sexy stranger? I decided to assume he was married and that I never had a chance anyway.

As I turned the key, I wondered if I would build up the nerve to return to these shops again in a couple of weeks, months... Eventually anyone who witnessed my tantrum would have forgotten what I looked like. In time, if I made this my new hangout, I might cross paths with the gorgeous stranger again. My behaviour had been incredibly embarrassing, so I was probably looking at quite some time for it to be completely forgotten. If he wasn't already spoken for, I doubted he was going to remain single for the whole next year, so that was it. In five minutes I had either ruined a potentially wonderful future or saved myself from a serial killer. I decided to assume that he was the latter so I had no excuse for regrets.

Driving along the tree-lined road, my head no longer thumped and the sheer beauty of low-hanging branches and manicured properties helped to ease my thirst. This was my favourite stretch of road during my commute to work. I could daydream of one day residing in such a pricey neighbourhood. The properties were huge: each driveway longer than an average house block. Apart from a lotto win, my chances of obtaining my dream were slim, but I was still young enough to believe that if I worked hard and saved, maybe one day I could get there. Though, to be honest, my wage wouldn't cover the power bills of these properties. There was no need to be sensible with my money – lotto was my only chance.

Even the birds were more attractive this side of the city. The flock of white birds flying towards me weren't seagulls or ducks; they were magnificent powder-white doves, and I had never seen anything so beautiful. I wondered if they had been released at a funeral – I had heard people did that. As they flew closer, I felt a calming presence as if I was about to be whisked off into the clouds to float above the world.

The calm turned to panic when I realised that they really were coming straight for me and, one after another, they dashed themselves against my windscreen. I'm not a religious person but the bloody, winged imprints, like scarlet angels, were terrifying. I swerved but they continued to come at me. Nothing I tried would discourage these birds from splattering onto my windscreen that became a dripping, red blinding shield. Completely bereft of any vision, I attempted to pull off the road but somehow, with no reasonable explanation, I planted my foot on the accelerator and ploughed straight into one of the trees I'd been admiring just moments earlier.

That earlier feeling of being whisked off into the clouds had become a reality, not that I felt calm looking down at my unconscious body slumped over the steering wheel. There was not a feather to be seen and my blood-splattered windscreen was spotless. If I was dead, why didn't the doves take me with them instead of leaving me floating in limbo? I had never believed in ghosts but now it seemed that I had become one. Beneath me, I heard a paramedic say that I was alive.

"No, I'm not," I screamed. "I'm up here floating. Get me down."
My screams were in vain. No-one heard a word I had spoken. I'd always imagined floating in air to be an amazing sensation, but instead of having the weight lifted from me, I was wracked with intense muscle contractions, unable to move so much as my little finger without fear of plummeting to the ground. After my earlier screams, I was afraid to even blink, so I had to watch as they calmly carried my body away on a stretcher. There was no attempt at CPR, nothing. These were either the most incompetent paramedics or something much stranger was going on. Unfortunately the latter turned out to be correct.

000-02-000

I AWOKE IN MY tiny unit without any memory of what had transpired the day before. Although small, my home was lovely, filled with gorgeous, comfortable furniture, an oversized television and a spare bedroom to store my clothes, decorator items and paintings that I just had to purchase.

One day I'd find a real place for them but at the moment they just didn't work with my furniture, and I couldn't have ornaments that didn't match on display. I had no problem with untidiness. People might see clothes draped over the furniture, but they were designer outfits so it was still in good taste.

Work itself was fairly mundane as always, but I received a decent wage for doing very little so I couldn't complain. I wasn't completely sure what the mechanical parts we sold were used for and I didn't need to know. With my phone manner and appearance, I covered the prerequisites for my position perfectly.

Appearance wasn't a requirement of the job, but I don't think mine hurt. I'm not model-type, jaw-dropping attractive, but I'm not overweight and I usually rate a second look. In a work place full of technically-inclined men, that came in very handy, especially when my car played up. I didn't have the interest or the money to buy a new one. My friends always carried on about my car not suiting my well-dressed image, but it spent its life in garages, used only to get me to work and back. I never had to drive anywhere else.

Emily and Jackie didn't like its unreliability, and Simone wouldn't be seen dead in it, giving me more than enough reason to never upgrade. My company also paid for my fuel, which was a wonderful perk. I used a company card, and on the many occasions that it didn't work at the service station, a quick phone call saved me from the highly embarrassing situation I saw so many others suffer.

"Sorry but your card has been declined – lack of funds," the cashier would say, leaving the customer trying to explain their predicament while a line of people waited impatiently behind them. If I had to hand over my own cards, I'd be constantly ringing my parents to retrieve me from the police station for purchasing fuel I couldn't afford, so I really couldn't complain about my job. Mind you, I always happily handed over those same cards at supermarkets and occasionally that embarrassing situation would arise but I had such a collection to go through I was generally covered. I suppose my fear came more from the fact that if I paid for my own fuel, there really would be no cards left to turn to because I seriously would have been out of money.

With night approaching, I was dressed to impress for no particular reason. It was just dinner with friends but my lift was so late, I'd had an extra hour to get ready. Simone was one of my closest friends but punctuality was not her thing. Her habit of being late for everything was incredibly frustrating, but after many years I had learnt to accept and deal with it. Her boyfriend, on the other hand, I just couldn't warm to. He was away so I was looking forward to a Bradley-free night.

Bradley – I used to like the name, now I cringed whenever I heard it. He had always been nice to me, and he was a great boyfriend to Simone so there was no reason for my dislike. He just happened to be one of those people who had the best of everything, from his designer suits, well-manicured nails and perfectly groomed hair that made Simone and I look like hobos in his presence. Well, more myself than her, because he couldn't possibly have a bedraggled looking girlfriend to parade around, but he did look prettier than her. Fine for a parrot!

He was constantly buying the newest, the latest, the have-not-been-released-to-the-low-life-public-yet purely, I felt, to rub our noses in it. His obsession with new gadgets would encourage him to buy many of the same items. Technology was moving so fast the upgraded version of most things turned up within months, and with three or more at home, Bradley still had to have the latest. This was occasionally quite the bonus for his friends, including me, as he sometimes handed us the old stuff – another reason I should have adored him.

What I think really annoyed me was that he knew all about everything, and everyone worth knowing. Well that's what he said. As I generally didn't have a clue about anyone he spoke of, I had to assume he was right. It was easier just to smile and nod. The only problem was that he never stopped talking about these elusive, important people, so I just couldn't stop myself considering him a conceited, cashed-up tool.

Simone finally arrived in a designer outfit. It was a weakness we shared as we loved to shop. Our taste was just not as exquisite as Bradley's. He must have had the gay friend we were lacking. Regardless, everyone needed a hobby, and shopping for beautiful clothes was ours. She had the cashed-up boyfriend to pay for it, and I had a lot of credit cards.

She pranced in, swinging her perfectly blow-waved blonde locks around, bellowing her excitement that Brad was going to make it to dinner after all. *Oh goody*, I thought, another night hearing about Brad's accomplishments. Unfortunately, that extra hour getting ready made me look way too good to stay home, so I just smiled, nodded to limber my neck up for the night and pretended to be happy for her.

The restaurant was full, with customers spilling through the door, so Simone strolled past everyone and flung herself at the maître d'.

"Booking for Lara," Simone interrupted, with no please or thank you.

"You're late," replied the maître d', unimpressed by her rudeness.

"Oh, I'm really sorry," she replied, now turning back into the considerate person I used to know and like. "I hope we didn't lose our place."

"No, your friends have been here for quite a while. Hopefully they are the forgiving type." He gave me a sly grin and led us to the table. Simone followed sheepishly. She was learning way too many bad habits from Bradley.

There they were – Mr and Mrs Reliable – Jackie and Dean. Seriously that was their name; well actually it was Trust but same thing. They were the most dependable, accommodating couple I knew. At one stage I seriously considered having my name legally changed to Elisha Wealthy or Elisha Smart but I couldn't decide which name I preferred, and to be honest, I was never really going to put in the effort to change it. So Elisha Dullard I would stay until the day I married a man with a more exciting last name. I truly blamed my name for my lack of motivation and boring existence, especially when Jackie and Dean suited their name so well.

The two of them were only a year older than me but they were so mature. Childhood sweethearts with their life mapped out to the last precise detail. They had married, bought a property, started a hairdressing business together – all at the exact time they had planned as teenagers. I was looking forward to the next few years when their baby plans were scheduled. I've heard that the getting-pregnant thing is a little hit and miss, but Jackie wasn't worried. She knew the dates and sex of each child she was planning to have. I decided if it turned out to be correct, she was a witch. I was going to have to keep my distance or be incredibly nice to her.

They were your picture-perfect couple in so many ways, from finishing each other's sentences to the smiles that appeared every time their eyes met. It was sometimes almost creepy, because they were those soppy love story movies that you never believed could be true. I'd almost guarantee that they would have perfectly well-behaved children, not the bratty ones causing havoc in stores like I was sure I would have if I ever bred – not that it was my intention – but if some accident did occur, I had already sized them up for the job of adoptive parents. Their calming attitude had already turned a once-psychotic Rottweiler into the most placid excuse for a dog I had ever met, so controlling my guaranteed-feral child would be a piece of cake for them. That was my parental plan anyway, and they were so nice that they offered to go along with it.

I couldn't help but grin slyly when I noticed Jackie and Dean sitting alone at a fairly large, but otherwise empty table. They actually looked a little lost in the large wooden chairs engulfing them.

"Would you like some friends?" I asked, as I took my oversized seat.

"Really not funny," replied Jackie in anger. "You're over an hour late."

While Simone pleaded her case, I just shrugged my shoulders and pointed her way. It was amusing watching the two of them criticise her behaviour. They would have made great schoolteachers, and I should have been hall monitor. I'll always blame someone else if it gets me out of trouble.

Next came the larger-than-life entrance of Bradley, explaining his own lack of punctuality. He always had an excuse for his tardiness because everything he did was so much more important than dinner with us. He worked in banking. It wasn't as if he was a surgeon out saving lives so his excuses were awfully thin. We all knew he just wanted everyone to notice his entrance – a fact made more obvious by his deflated demeanour on noticing the absence of Emily and Justin. It was well worth a silent snigger to myself as it was incredibly rare to see Bradley feel uncomfortable.

"They've broken up," said Dean, shocking us all.

"Emily's around somewhere," added Jackie. "She's on the phone talking to him and it was getting a bit heated, so she's obviously gone off looking for somewhere a little more private." That really took the shine off for Bradley. The night wasn't going to be about him after all.

It turned out that Justin had committed the ultimate sin on a drunken night out with the boys and was found in bed with a red head the next morning. There was no way Emily would accept that behaviour, and I was a little surprised to hear that she was actually talking to him at all. She had cut others off completely for a lot less. Emily hadn't been with Justin for long but it was a good few months, which was impressive for her, and he seemed nice enough.

Emily was an extremely confident female, like Jackie, and I often wondered if it had something to do with their darker hair shade. Simone and I never seemed to exude great intelligence as they often did, adding credence to the dumb blonde theory. Except for the fact that Simone was actually a brunette in disguise and, in many circumstances, thicker than me, I would have accepted the theory as gospel. Simone hadn't been any cleverer before she discovered bleach – she actually seemed to get smarter with it.

Emily had a great job that she loved and spent half of her life travelling solo to third-world jungles that clear thinking humans would be clever enough to avoid. The best way to determine Emily's next holiday destination was to check the government warnings on Google, and if it read 'Do Not Travel', it was a fair bet that was where she was heading. We often mentioned this to her and occasionally Simone and I would take bets before asking, but she ignored us completely and left us behind, eagerly anticipating her return. I'm not sure Justin ever shared her spirit for adventure so the relationship was possibly always doomed to fail.

Emily finally appeared with a rare look of panic upon her face, shaking a little as she first dropped her phone, then grabbed it and threw it with force onto the table. I never expected to see fear on the face of this woman. She was a powerhouse of confidence and strength, completely devoid of weak emotions like anxiety and fear. If something was rattling her, it must have been horrendous.

"He's stalking me. He has access to all my cards. He just told me everything I had done for the last week and almost everywhere I've been and he said if I don't see him, he knows how to cancel the cards."

"So use cash!" I jumped in with what I thought to be an easy solution to her problem and a way for me to be the clever one for a change.

"Really!" said Jackie in disbelief. "Cash has been out of circulation for over a year."

That killed my bright idea. She was right and I knew it, but it seemed like yesterday it was still legal tender. Emily, on the other hand, was appreciative of my comment. I had opened the floodgates for her to give us another reason why she hated this new cashless society.

"Haven't you noticed the new charges on your cards – the ones I warned you about," she said passionately, forgetting her ex-boyfriend troubles for a moment. "I told you it would happen. First they made it hard for you to use cash, charging exorbitant amounts to pay your bills with it or use ATMs. Now you're getting charged for every transaction you make with a card and why? Because now you have no other choice. Just like I told you all."

"You can use your phone," jumped in Simone.

"And that will be charged next, you idiot. Seriously, are you all that dumb?" replied Emily. "Especially you, Simone! When's the last time your phone was fully charged enough to use it anywhere?" It was an attack Simone should have seen coming, but as I said before, she was generally dumber than me.

"No, last time I was with you I couldn't use it because I'd lost it again. Remember!" replied Simone, not realising the repercussions of her comment.

"You lost it!" began Emily. "At least out of battery no-one could empty your bank account."

"It's alright. I don't let her set it up for banking," jumped in Bradley, "because we know how forgetful she is with it." That didn't help their cause.

"You're a bunch of idiots," Emily interrupted. "You put your entire lives in the hands of the banks. Remember these institutions have been doing you over for years, changing the rules as it suited them. Now your behaviour has not only put my life in their hands, but also into the hands of Justin. So thanks, guys. Thanks a fucking lot."

Emily wasn't one to mince her words. For those she offended who didn't know her, it was just easier to explain her behaviour by suggesting that she must have been the victim of some mystical spell. Whenever a thought entered her mind, good, bad or just nasty, it quickly gushed straight from her mouth. There was no time wasted thinking about whether or not it was appropriate to say, and it generally wasn't, but with Emily it was just said and to be honest, that's what I really admired about her. She was also usually right. We were that ignorant. She had warned us many times about the hole we were digging for ourselves but it was just so easy to hand over a piece of plastic, for me especially. I liked buying things I couldn't really afford. The end of the month was always a problem when I realised how much I'd spent, but the idea of having savings was never part of my grand plan.

I remembered back to the days of cash when Emily and I dropped into a supermarket to buy some junk food for a big film night. Excited about the evening ahead, I quickly handed over my card to pay the cashier and unwisely declined the receipt she offered me. The second we walked through the sliding doors into the blizzard-like conditions of the car park, Emily attacked me. It was like I had just skied down the slopes haphazardly, happy to have made it through, but was now facing off with a snow wolf. Was she going to eat me or just growl about my poor descent?

"How much did that cost?" Emily asked, in a tone I knew was the beginning of another lecture, whatever my answer. She was intending to go in for the kill.

"About twenty-five dollars," I answered, praying that I was at least close to the right amount.

"Thirty-eight dollars and ninety-five cents," she said disapprovingly. "You're obviously wealthy enough to ignore thirteen dollars and ninety-five cents." Annoyed by her quick calculation, I just suggested that it wasn't that much.

"No, but do that seven times a week, and you're ninety-seven dollars and sixty-five cents over your estimated budget."

I'd never thought of it that way, mostly because I don't have a calculator in my head, or a budget for that matter, but she didn't stop there.

"Knowing you, I'd assume that you're generally even more off on your calculations and probably about twenty-five dollars off on most of your purchases, making you one hundred and seventy-five dollars in the red. So it seems you are doing financially better in life than you thought. I know I couldn't handle being nearly two hundred dollars out every week. Lucky you don't need a receipt to check your spending." A cheap shot because she knew I was always out of money before my next pay, clever wolf that she was. Emily just wanted us all to use cash, especially me, so I'd stop getting into trouble because I could only spend what I could see. I'm not sure what possessed me to even try and fight back, but I thought I could possibly beat her for once and gave it a shot.

"If I carried around cash I'd probably just get robbed, so it's safer this way."

"Would you carry around a thousand dollars in your wallet?"

"No," I replied, a little scared of where she was going with this.

"So if someone stole your purse and card with its cool tap and go – no need for a pin or signature technology – they could have spent a thousand dollars before you even noticed it was gone."

"That's alright. The bank would just replace the money. They wouldn't replace cash." That had to have covered me, I thought. I'd outsmarted the vicious canine.

"They might eventually return it to you when you prove it was stolen, leaving you with a really small budget until your next payday. Then you would have to wait for a replacement card or you could have maybe just lost fifty dollars, not a thousand. And, let's be honest, you misplace ninety-odd a week now. My point is if you're not going to use cash, can you at least get a receipt so you know what the hell you're spending?"

"I can just look it up online."

"So basically you are putting all of your trust into your bank, an institution that has never done wrong by you? If they say you spent it, they must be right, even though I remember them taking three months and many phone calls to return the three hundred dollars you accidently paid twice when the machine scanned the other card in your wallet." She was right, that did happen but they eventually fixed it.

"And I'm fairly sure I've heard you complain about the strange descriptions for some of your purchases that you just couldn't remember making but you had no receipts or proof to even check yourself. Don't forget that these are the institutions that continually change the rules to suit themselves, adding unexpected transaction fees to accounts that originally had none and increasing interest rates when you least expect it just to appease their shareholders or, more importantly, CEOs or Bradleys." I noticed her little addition and just gave a sly, I-get-what-you-mean grin. "You know the ones that you constantly complain about. It makes complete sense that you would leave all your finances in their capable hands. You could at least get the bank's spend-tracking app."

I just gave a nod with a smile. All this was because I didn't take the receipt. She could have at least waited till we got to the car to lecture me, but Emily didn't work like that. And, to be honest, I was just relieved she at least waited until we'd walked out of the shop – not a usual habit of hers.

Emily truly loved her cash and hated the rest of us using cards, so a shopping trip with her could embarrass or mentally scar me for days. If it wasn't about us using cash or getting receipts, there was her passionate disdain for self-service.

On one occasion we'd had a wonderful day shopping up a storm. Our trolleys overflowed with what we had been programmed to believe were great bargains – gorgeous dresses, shoes, make-up, face creams and the occasional, just-had-to-have designer ornaments.

Emily was a brilliant bargain hunter, showing me the true meaning of a fun day out with fairly limited funds. This time I even played along, keeping track of how much I was spending, plugging the price of every item into my phone calculator. I used to giggle a little when I watched others tallying their spending in supermarkets, thinking you geeky loser. Now I was one of them and it seriously curtailed my need for those extra things I would have purchased before and never used.

Unfortunately I never had the courage to shop that way alone or with Simone, or with anyone but Emily for that matter. She didn't feel geeky doing it, so with her, I didn't either. I tried it once with my mother.

"What are doing? You're embarrassing me!" she said, "Put that calculator away." Thanks for the support, Mum, I thought. I didn't bother saying it out loud as she generally paid the bill anyway. Really, she should have encouraged my attempt at sensible behaviour, seeing as she was always the one getting me out of financial trouble. When she didn't realise that, I understood where my capacity for bad decisions came from.

My day out with Emily had been amazing until we arrived at the cashier. This particular store was obviously short-staffed so the lines were a little long, but funnily enough so were the self-service lines next to us – a fact not lost on Emily.

"Idiots!" Emily declared loudly. "Their excuse for using an unstaffed checkout is because they're supposedly in a hurry, and the morons are going to be here longer than us." Naturally the morons heard us and the evil stares in our direction were upsetting my previously perfect day. Then a large woman with a young daughter in her pram decided to respond to Emily's bantering. As soon as she opened her mouth, I could feel the hair on Emily's neck prickling, and there was a trolley between us. I wanted to say, "shut up, fat lady", but I doubt that would have calmed the situation.

"I like to serve myself because I prefer the way that I pack my items, and there's no suffering ridiculous small talk with cashiers," the woman said defensively to Emily. This was never going to get me out of there and to safety any time soon.

"I doubt that you pack your bags better than a professional," replied Emily. "And with small talk being beneath you, I'm sure the cashiers are as relieved as you are. I just find it amazing that you don't care about the future of your daughter or her friends ever having the opportunity to find a part-time job because there soon won't be any with people like you serving yourself."

"My daughter will never be a check-out chick!" the woman replied, insinuating this to be beneath her, which really didn't suit her cheap lipstick or the bargain-basement store we were situated in.

"So you get my point!" replied Emily with a smile, completely disregarding the woman's tone. "The days of customer service will soon become a distant memory." The lady didn't bother replying. She seemed uncertain as to whether she had been insulted or not. Emily was quite clever at doing that to people. I saw several shoppers change lanes to the cashier after her tirade.

Emily meant well because, to her, self-service meant the loss of jobs for so many that depended on them. As she too worked in a service industry, she feared the future that was now presenting itself and was baffled by the general public's apparent disregard. The supermarkets always said it didn't take away jobs but, as Emily often pointed out, that one staff member watching ten people serve themselves was one person doing the job of ten, maybe five, but either number still meant less staff were needed.

She was right, but like everyone else I found the way she explained it offensive. Besides, I was always in a hurry and didn't want to wait in line. Knowing Emily's passion, I continued to use self-service without her around. I just did it instinctively and I wasn't planning on having children anyway or, if I did, I was giving them to Jackie so what harm could it do to me? Simone would just explain that Bradley and her future children would be rich and not need a part-time job, so there was no reason for her to use the cashier either. That's what Simone told me that she'd told Emily, but I very much doubt she had said a word. Like myself, she never self-served around Emily.

Another time with Emily, we entered a small bakery that only accepted cash. The customer ahead of us wasn't at all happy about the situation. Even I found it a little ridiculous watching the man try to hand over his card for a two-dollar donut. When the cashier informed him that there was an ATM across the street, he erupted into a fully-fledged tantrum, loudly ranting that he would never enter their shop again because it was beneath him to have to pay cash, and, as a business, it was their responsibility to accommodate him. Luckily for the cashier, Emily was more than happy to take him on.

"You rude prick," she began, seriously making me wonder if I was going to survive this day at all. The fact that he was triple our size didn't seem to daunt her in the least. With her head almost tilted backwards, she attempted to stare him in the eye, a feat she was at least a foot off accomplishing. "You expect this tiny shop to pay extra money to a greedy bank to supply their machines just so you don't have to cross the road and take out a couple of dollars. It's not like the exercise would hurt you and, if they give into your kind, that same item is going to cost more money because if they do it your way it's certainly going to cost them. The banks charge businesses for doing their work, not the other way around."

"Sorry," said the now not-so-scary man, probably just shocked into submission. "I'm just not used to carrying cash around."

"Yeah, and we're all going to pay for that one day. Trust me on that." Emily finished with the last word again as the man disappeared from the shop, obviously amazed that he had copped abuse from a female he could probably have squashed with his elbow.

If Emily's ranting wasn't enough, she had another trick up her sleeve in the days when we still had cash. With long lines of patrons waiting to be served and getting all annoyed when they saw someone take cash from their wallet, Emily would slowly pay at the counter with coins just to frustrate and annoy the card users behind her and embarrass the hell out of me.

When I say coins, I mean small coins that take a long time to count out, especially when the purchase was over twenty dollars. Mostly dollar coins, but just enough fives and tens to make everyone's life unpleasant. She always seemed to have an endless supply of them. I don't know how she carried them; she obviously had very strong shoulders. Her bad behaviour possibly backfired and helped encourage the changes that followed, but I wasn't going to be the one to ever tell her that.

To be fair, Emily had many good reasons to despise the new cashless society, and one particular incident gave her every excuse in the world to have strong views. A couple of years earlier, with the world economy just moving away from cash, a terrifyingly evil incident occurred.

Her older sister April was driving home from work one night when her car broke down on a desolate country road. Living away from the city with very limited public transport, we assume she would have been relieved when she saw one of the few public buses coming her way.

Home was a good hour's walk away and her mobile was completely flat, leaving her no way to reach her husband or friends who could have picked her up. We could only imagine her despair when the bus driver explained that he couldn't take her aboard because she couldn't pay for her fare. She had money but the only way to take public transport was with one of their cards, which could not be purchased on the bus.

April had never needed to take public transport since moving away from town, and the last time she had used it she could give the bus driver a few dollars and catch a ride. She probably had no idea that was no longer an option. I never met April but, knowing her sister, I imagine she would not have taken this news well. So there was poor April, miles from home and her only safe way of getting there was not possible.

Emily assumed that after throwing a tantrum, April would have felt that her only option was to hitchhike. They used to do it for fun when they were teenagers, so how dangerous could it really be? We don't really know if she hitchhiked or not. It was completely irrelevant because, regardless of thumbing a ride or not, she was alone in the dark on a quiet road with nothing to defend herself. She could not have avoided the outcome. Her lifeless body was found a few days later in a dam with enough stab wounds to have killed her twenty times over. She would have made it home safely on the bus but she'd been robbed of that simple life-saving option.

To save her parents or inconsolable husband the heartache of identifying April, Emily decided it was her duty and I offered to accompany her. Not a clever move by me as it was the most horrendous thing I'd ever seen. To try to protect us, they had only left the smallest amount of her face uncovered – it didn't help. Her blood-soaked hair couldn't hide the stab wounds covering her face.

I don't know how she could tell but Emily quickly identified April then ran to toilet where she spent twenty minutes vomiting. I wanted to do something but what could I say that was ever going to fix this. There was no upside, no comforting words. I just cried along with her, hoping she could find a way to move on one day. It was the right decision, Emily seemed to cope with the nightmare and my silence had saved me from any chance of saying the wrong thing.

As for the effect on me, to be honest, April didn't look human anymore. It reminded me of one of the B-grade movies I had seen where make-up artists had tried so hard to make something look scary, it no longer looked real. In my head I hadn't seen a tortured human, just a really bad movie prop, and that's how I managed to sleep at night. Eventually, the three men arrested said that she was hitchhiking, but since they had raped and murdered her, their version was never going to be reliable. Only the fact that she had fought so hard to save her own life, leaving the men covered in easily identifiable bite marks, lead to their capture. The DNA under her fingernails guaranteed their fast arrest, conviction and imprisonment.

April had endured a horrific death from three of the lowest lifeforms to ever walk this earth and, meeting her two young children at her funeral, I quickly understood why she'd put up such a fight. Watching her husband trying to be strong for his babies gave me an uncomfortable insight into the feelings she must have been going through. I could only imagine her trying to wipe the pain by thinking of her family, doing everything in her limited power to get back to them. To know she would never see them again was probably the greatest trauma she suffered. Emily had always spoken of how happy they were. All destroyed now and avoidable if only she could have caught that bus. The fact that with cash in her hand she was unable to do that caused Emily no end of pain.

It didn't just end with the destruction of one family; the bus driver too became a victim, blaming himself and taking his own life three days later. The media reports focussed on the murdered hitchhiker aspect, implying somehow the victim was at fault. The whole bus incident was never mentioned. It made no sense that a young mother was raped and tortured by three psychopaths and the media only mentioned it in passing, omitting the terrifying details. Something one would have assumed to be front page news was nothing more than a tiny snippet.

The family only became aware of the public transport tragedy after the bus driver's distraught wife contacted April's parents to tell them of her husband's inconsolable guilt and suicide. Both families tried in vain to have the truth reported but they were constantly ignored. Emily encouraged us all to spread the real story on Facebook, Twitter and any form of social media we could think of, but nothing eventuated. Our posts disappeared almost as quickly as we typed them. We would have garnered more attention with a picture of an ugly cat. Emily certainly had a lot to be angry about.

Now Emily had broken up with, and was being stalked by, a man who was computer savvy – a dangerous problem in a cashless new world.

000-03-000

WITHOUT CASH, DETAILS OF every transaction you made were now available to anyone clever enough to look. Fine if you didn't make any computer nerd enemies, incredibly scary if you did. That's not actually true because you didn't really need to annoy a knowledgeable computer hacker, being downright unlucky could easily bring them straight to you. Just opening one of the thousand emails you received each day could be enough to give them the access they needed to wipe you clean, and they often did. Many of the scammers were overseas so they were never caught. Technology that brought the world to us all inadvertently brought the criminals with it.

Security could never really keep up with the hackers so, like the many others, Justin had a wonderful time, easily managing to track every move Emily made, revelling in being able to tell her about the donut she had two days ago and expressing surprise at how much she had spent on a purse. He wanted her back, and he was intending to make her life hell until she returned to him. He told her that being able to track her movements was only part of the fun because his next step was going to be emptying her bank accounts. Her annoying predictions had materialised, but not the way that she had envisioned. She had wasted her breath explaining to us how the government and large institutions could track our every move, how they could pinpoint all of our transactions, knowing where we had been, what we were doing, what we ate, drank and anything else we purchased. She'd never considered that a nasty ex-boyfriend could do the same.

We should not have doubted her predictions. Even with cash still in circulation, we were encouraged to use reward cards for our day-to-day shopping. They cost us nothing and occasionally gave us something back, like a discount. Even Emily was happy to have them for her favourite stores. Because scanning that card whenever you shopped gave them an exact picture of everything you purchased, they would email you when products you liked were on sale. Still nothing to be concerned about. I didn't care if they knew what I had bought and, to be honest, neither did Emily. She did, however, occasionally worry about the ramifications of this new type of technology. The supermarkets used it to encourage you to buy more of the products that you liked anyway, so who cared. For me it was win, win. The fact that the supermarkets now knew that you bought a lot of condoms, way too many painkillers or, in my case, chocolate was irrelevant, I thought. And it was – until the choice was taken away.

Without cash you could no longer decide when to scan that card. As no-one had cash they now knew everything about you. Loyalty cards were gone because they didn't need to offer you anything in return. They had your information regardless, and so did anyone else who could work out how to get it. Privacy was a thing of the past in this new cash-free world. Everything was out there for anyone to find, unfortunately including Justin.

Emily had immediately informed the police about Justin's hacking, but we all knew he was going to be one step ahead of them, leaving us with no idea how to help her. A room full of friends about as useful as a discarded sock. Even the great, all-knowing Bradley had no answers for Emily, and neither did Jackie, the responsible adult type who kept us all in check. She generally told us things to make us feel better and to find ways to improve our situation but without actually eradicating the problem.

Emily was the true fixer in our group because she didn't care about silly things like our feelings. If I asked, "Do I look fat in this?" Simone would just shrug, Jackie would fiddle with the outfit, but Emily would give me the answer I actually needed.

"Yes! You look ridiculous. Throw it away or go on a diet."

It was never a good idea to ask her opinion if you weren't up to hearing the truth, but if you needed help, she was the only one who could really give it. If she didn't know what to do about this Justin situation, it was a fair bet that no-one did.

When the time came for paying the bill, the waiter walked around with a magnetic stripe reader to scan our cards or phones. The old days of having the bill dropped on the table, leaving us to work out who owed what, was a lot more interesting. Emily would always grab the bill as she was our human calculator and just tell each of us what we owed, including the appropriate tip. She never appreciated relinquishing her duty and informed us that now the restaurants had to take on her job, they were certainly charging for it – on each transaction, not just once for the whole table. She knew this because she worked at one of these restaurants.

I also remember a little trick that used to occur when I went out for dinner with work colleagues occasionally. We didn't have Emily so the bill would be handed around from person to person. Everyone often put in a little extra so, by the time it got to the last person, they could almost receive a free meal. That person was often me. I'm sure that everyone knew what was happening because they generally made me last, knowing that my wage was minimal in comparison to theirs, and when someone on a lower wage than me was at the table, they'd get the bill. That scenario and occasional free meal disappeared with the end of cash, taking the shine off my work dinners.

When the waiter scanned my card, it was rejected. I hadn't brought any backups to cover myself because I had been trying to behave and only use the card connected to my account. Unfortunately I'd forgotten about my electricity bill coming out and my pay hadn't gone through yet. I'd been trying really hard to keep a record of my spending so a couple of dollars would have been all that I was out. That didn't matter because if the card didn't go through, I couldn't pay my bill and I guessed that embarrassing moment would be remembered for years. I had a problem of keeping track of my bills. Every one of them was buried in the fifty-odd emails I received daily. I was positive that some email bills from my power and phone company didn't always turn up. I had no real idea when they were due but often the money would just disappear from my account, forcing me to go through the many old emails – unable to find them. When I did ring and mention that I didn't even receive my bill, they would just say that their records said it was sent and it was my problem to deal with my internet provider who pretended to fix it, but it would happen again. I never complained too much because I knew I wasn't computer literate, so somehow it must have been my fault. I never mentioned it to my friends because I found the whole process a little embarrassing and I thought I must have been the only one this happened to because I never heard them complain. There were no longer the handy pieces of paper I could put on the fridge, another of Emily's predictions becoming reality, as the world had become addicted to email, Facebook and other social media to keep in touch rather than the old-fashioned way of sending things or writing a letter. I'm not that sure that this new technology was really the demise of the handwritten letter. To be honest, not even my parents sent letters. They just spoke to their friends over the phone so its end was predictable regardless.

The real problems began when companies decided that paying postage was no longer cost effective, so why not just send out your bill electronically. For them it was great as it was free. Of course they chose not to share these savings with their customers but instead charged those who preferred to be sent a bill. Even the Government encouraged people to avoid the state-owned postal service, apparently too stupid to realise that they were the ones that profited from it. Instead of encouraging people to use the post, they decided to put up the price of postage and took longer to deliver it, forcing those who were still posting invoices and letters to make the switch to email. Interesting way to attract customers by lowering service standards and charging more for them, only a government could come up with such an unreasonable business model. Mind you, the postal service's main source of revenue was now due to the huge amounts of online shopping it now had the pleasure of charging to deliver. Soon post offices too began disappearing, and the many jobs associated with them.

Not everybody had a computer with an email account so companies found that they could triple the price of posting out their bills, so they did. The world had been forced to join the computer age, which for some was not the easy option as internet connection wasn't free and in some communities it was almost inaccessible.

I lived close to the city and continually had connection problems, and every time I phoned a government agency or large company their excuse for taking so long was always blamed on their computer system. Children were unable to complete their homework without it. Due to the diminishing job situation Emily was warning us about, there were a lot of families living below the poverty line who had to come up with new, inventive ways to survive, like buying second-hand tablets and parking close to fast-food restaurants to use their free wi-fi.

Libraries, the once-preferred place to comfortably use free internet, had all but disappeared. Now people were unable to receive their basic bills without an internet connection. It didn't bother the power companies because they just took the money from bank accounts and, if the money wasn't available, the power was cut off. Left with empty bank accounts and no heat or power, the less fortunate were soon becoming the completely forgotten.

The things Emily had predicted were actually coming true, but we still refused to heed her advice. We were losing the element of choice. We'd let it slip away for what we thought, or were told, was our convenience, not even noticing the many times that it wasn't. Emily saw it coming but, if she couldn't even convince her friends, there was no way it was going to change back.

I tried taking Emily's advice and printing the bills up myself when they came, but once the ink ran out on my printer, I stopped. Buying a printer I didn't particularly want was one thing, paying out ridiculous prices for the ink was just not going to happen. As always the case, my stupidity came back to bite me. I had just given good old Bradley the chance to be the hero again as he quickly rushed in to cover my bill. To prove his greatness he offered to cover dinner for everyone. Seriously I should have loved this guy, and I'm so glad that I never told anybody that I didn't.

Bradley proudly ran his fist along the scanner, shocking everyone, including the waiter, especially when it worked.

"What have you done?" asked Emily, absolutely horrified by what she had just witnessed.

Bradley excitedly explained how he was one of the first to test this amazing new technology. A barcode had been tattooed onto his hand and that was now all that he would ever need to pay for anything.

"You have the mark!" exclaimed Emily in horror. "The devil's mark!"

I know Emily wasn't Bradley's greatest fan but mark of the devil was probably a little extreme.

Emily then proceeded to explain that her many years spent at a Christian school gave her plenty of time to peruse the Bible, and she was most surprised that none of us had any knowledge of the stories.

She was wrong. I knew all about the Baby Jesus. I loved Christmas with the Christ in it, and I'd watched films about Moses and stuff. She didn't appreciate my input and it wasn't good enough to stop her continuing.

"Revelation," she insisted, "It's all in Revelation. You need to read it. It's too late for you, Bradley. You just bought yourself a ticket straight to hell."

Now my friend was really starting to scare me. I'd never seen her go to church – I didn't think she had a religious bone in her body. The way she carried on I felt like calling the Feds to arrest her. I was a little afraid of her going the way of a god-bothering terrorist and pulling out a gun to knock off Bradley. I may not have been his greatest fan but even I felt that murdering him was probably a little extreme. She did say Bible, the favourite book of many a madman through the ages. Nowadays I was pretty sure that the Quran was the terrorist maker – another book psychopaths could hijack to suit their lunatic agenda. So it seemed there was no need to call for backup as she was referring to the other book, the one people no longer excused or accepted bad behaviour relating to.

Emily explained to us in no uncertain terms that the Bible tells that before the end of time, people will take a mark on their right hand or forehead, and it will become the only form of currency. Those without will suffer immensely for their remaining time on Earth, but for those with it, it will be the mark of the beast and they will be destined to spend eternity in the flaming pits of hell. What a fun way to end the night it was, but Emily was under a lot of stress so we felt that her rant should be forgiven. Like parents disregarding a child's ramblings, we all gave her a friendly hug goodbye and a pat on the head. We had no idea what she was talking about but it didn't matter because we loved her anyway. Unfortunately, she wasn't a child and didn't appreciate being patronised.

"Yeah, you can all go fuck yourselves," was her parting comment and, to be honest, I was happy that with all that was going on for her, she hadn't lost that up-yours spirit.

The barcode really shouldn't have surprised us at all. Even during the days of cash, they had been testing fingerprint and eye-scanning technology. Those impressive three-dimensional printers soon showed them their failings, being able to create exact copies of even full human faces. If a computer could store it, a printer could now recreate it. Voice recognition too was easily corrupted as the voices needed to be stored, making them easily accessible to criminals with the technology to copy and reuse. Emily's evil mark was probably destined for the same eventual demise, so I wasn't sure that she needed to become so aggressive to Bradley.

I had originally assumed the big phone companies played some part in the whole scenario as they were leading the charge to a cashless society but this new technology was soon going to lessen their grip.

Eventually, and against Emily's wishes, cash had been disposed of all together because so few were using it. Even though there was a minority that did, there were not enough of them to warrant the expense of actually manufacturing it. The non-cash users campaigned for its abolition on the grounds that it was only necessary for criminals and tax avoidance, which I considered a fairly legitimate reason. Emily, of course, didn't agree and spent hours trying to change our opinions.

Her first gripe, as she worked in the service industry, was the end of people tipping her colleagues, something that annoyed her immensely. Wait staff were on a low wage for the hours they had to work on nights and weekends, and she knew that the tips often made up for their inconvenience. Eventually, after consultation with her superiors – or, more likely, she just told them what she was doing – a service charge was added into the price.

What she enjoyed most about her price hike for customers was the fact that she had actually made the service charge more than most customers would have tipped, and she was now forcing those that hadn't to tip indirectly.

Her staff also knew that although service was still important to keep the customers coming in, there was really no need to go that extra mile anymore because the tips were the same regardless. Fortunately for Emily her restaurant was large and well known so, unlike her smaller competitors, she could get away with a lot more. It was the happiest I had seen her for a long time – finding a way to fight back against the system she hated – excited in the knowledge that she was charging more money for less customer service. Unfortunately, she could only gloat to us and her staff as her customers seemed to have no idea that they were being taken advantage of. Even when I explained to her that she had done well out of this cashless society, I wasn't met with the happy agreement I had anticipated.

"You've actually seen less drugs and crime?" she asked, already knowing the answer I had to give her.

I didn't bother answering because she was right. There was actually a lot more crime. The drug dealers were obviously having a wonderful time with this new cashless world as they'd always been a step ahead of authorities. The lack of cash wasn't going to change it now. They just came up with new inventive ways of selling their products by calling it different names and laundering their money through other countries that were now seeing the value in helping out the world's drug lords. Your two-bit dealer on the street now stood there with a scanner, the funds going directly offshore and returning to the dealer in a way that still somehow avoided the government's watch.

Nothing was real anymore – it was just numbers floating in cyberspace. They couldn't deal with the drug problem when there was something physical like cash to find. Now with that cash represented by numbers floating through the air, it seemed to make it impossible. Other types of criminals also found this new way more exciting because now, rather than rip someone off for a couple of dollars they may have had on them, they were getting access to entire bank accounts, and half the time they didn't even need to physically rob them. The smart ones just sat at home and hacked into people's accounts. It was only beginners who had to lower themselves to pickpocketing. They'd still have access to your accounts, but if you were quick and actually knew that you had been robbed, you could cancel the cards before too much damage had been done.

The threat of physical attack never disappeared as promised; it seemed there were now even more reasons to be mugged. One could still be a computer-illiterate thug and take all your belongings to any number of computer hackers to find someway of emptying your accounts and syphoning the money into their own account. They also found it in their best interest to leave you needing a trip straight to hospital, giving them extra time before you could cancel anything.

There was also a huge black market for stolen cars and other personal items, and just paying petty criminals with food, drugs or other stolen items seemed to encourage a whole new class of them to appear. The government now had precise personal details of each and every one of us so you would have thought that these criminals would have been so much easier to track down. But it must have been harder because there were more bad people out there and less of them being caught. It seemed as if the criminals were more computer literate than the authorities, and in this new world where we were so reliant on technology, they were the winners.

So Emily was right. With less employment there was a lot more crime and a considerably larger amount of the population on drugs. The tax-avoiding tradesmen and small businesses didn't seem too upset because all it meant for them was that they had the ability to always charge more for their service. The ones who had earlier complained about them had been the ones wanting a discount and they were now being charged the full price, probably plus some, like Emily did, so they too were generally the only losers.

What they had failed to realise was that asking the self-employed for a discount was like their boss telling them to take a pay cut. Accepting cash was the only way for the self-employed not to take a pay cut and still give a discount. The few hundred dollars in tax the government thought it had been losing never actually appeared as the tradesmen and anyone who had something to trade now made a lucrative living bartering.

Governments were receiving much less and the world was reverting back to the dark ages. Emily had always told us that, but we didn't believe it until we found out the hard way. A handyman I had always just handed cash over to when he came to fix my leaking taps and change my light globes, all of a sudden cost a lot more. I'd never asked for a discount but as he never arrived with a terminal to take a card, I just made sure to keep some cash handy. With no cash he had to arrive with a card-scanning terminal, and trust me, that brought the price up considerably.

Bradley was the most vocal in wanting to see the end of cash, so it was only fitting that it probably cost him more than any of us. He thought himself the master of getting a good price from tradesmen. He was actually far from it, and he suffered the most when he couldn't get a better deal without it. To be honest, I don't really think he was ever given a good deal but, without cash, he was given even less. I know that I wouldn't give a good price to someone that flashed his wealth around so much, and I would be really surprised if anyone else did. His watch was worth more than most people's cars. Where did he get off asking for a discount?

With Big Brother now in full force, of course only able to really track down the compliant general public, people were getting taxed on selling anything. There was no more selling second-hand stuff on eBay tax-free because if you sold anything now, it was taxed. It always baffled me how the government could tax all the law-abiding citizens for selling so little, but they still couldn't work out how to nab the criminals. It seriously inspired one to turn to crime – I so wished I hadn't been such a goody goody.

Garage sales too were a thing of the past because not everybody had the ability to scan potential customers, and they would have to pay tax on selling their old junk. The streets were becoming full of people's unwanted items. Old couches and furniture littered the streets, sometimes a good score if one could beat the vermin to it, but with so much out there and so much vermin, it was unlikely.

Emily once asked me to help her retrieve a beautiful, antique chair that was obviously in need of refurbishment. I helped her load it into her car, actually hoping that she would decide that she didn't like it, because it was really nice. I would have been happy to take it. Abandoned down the road the night before, we thought that it would still be in reasonable condition because it hadn't rained. Unfortunately the rats thought the same. I'm just relieved I didn't sit on it. As I pressed down, obviously disturbing the new resident, it jumped through the tiny rip and bit my finger. It was as horrifying as you could imagine. A dog, a stray cat, I could have handled but a rat, no – she was taking me straight to the hospital. They really did just give me a band-aid as she predicted. I still thought it was very rude of her to try to avoid taking me there just because she still needed my help picking up the chair. She actually returned for it with some other sucker, and she was correct – there had only been the one rat in it. I never got a sorry for the horrible situation she had made me endure, just abuse for being so pathetic about it. I was bitten by a rat and fairly convinced that I would be forever haunted by the incident.

It had now become irrelevant if you sold an item for less or more than its original price because the government found it too hard to distinguish so, for them, there was just a tax across the board. Even those people who were happy for cash to end or those, like myself, who didn't care either way were starting to realise that perhaps it wasn't such a good idea. Crime and tax evasion didn't cease – they only became a larger problem – but those legitimate little people like me who weren't clever enough to find ways to get around things were getting done over in every way.

I used to occasionally make a few dollars by selling my excess clothes and shoes online for nowhere near the price I had originally paid. Not that any cash ever changed hands – the money would just show up in my account. Now it was being taxed, the losses made it not worth the effort. Now people just exchanged items but I didn't want other people's old stuff so I just threw whatever I didn't want in the bin. I should have taken it to a charity shop but I didn't know of one close, so it wasn't an option.

I really felt sorry for the children – there was no point in their lemonade stands and car washes. The most they could now hope to gain were sweets that their parents would generally stop them eating. So the young entrepreneurs all disappeared from the street corners, and I missed the sweet pink lemonade I'd become accustomed to on a Saturday morning. The sellers had been so cute I didn't care that it was mostly sugar water with a squeeze of lemon. Occasionally children would use a phone to accept payment, but with the charge attached to each transaction, the lemonade stands soon disappeared for good.

Emily had been right again and we may have even apologised to her for not heeding her warnings, but I knew I couldn't handle her having that over me so I guessed the others couldn't either. Emily always knew that she was right. I don't think anyone agreeing with her would have made her a nicer person. She would have just become unbearable and lauded it over us.

As Emily predicted, basic postal services soon disappeared altogether. If you wanted to send a 'Xmas' card it was now charged at the more expensive parcel rate, retiring that old tradition too.

Sorry, it used to be called a Christmas card but political correctness ruled that out. The Christian religion wasn't followed by all, so rather than offend the other religions or atheists, it was decided that the word Christ could no longer be used, which annoyed even me because everyone was happy to take a holiday, but chose to forget Christ was the only reason we had the celebration.

Emily had suggested that this new attack on Christianity was part of a larger plan to sneak their mark through unnoticed. She may have been correct.

W HAT ANNOYED EMILY THE most was the fact that we were being forced to change our ways for people who had moved to western countries for a better way of life, a way of life that evolved from Christian values – principles that seemed fairly simple: don't kill, don't steal. Basic commonsense rules to live by. So if Christianity offended people with different religious beliefs, what could possibly have enticed them to move to a place based on it? I didn't really get religion but I certainly understood Emily's point. The countries they came from would undoubtedly not have returned the favour to Christians, so why should we care who our way of life upset? They could always just leave, another wonderful bonus of the western world, freedom to choose where one lived, just not how to receive or pay a bill anymore.

Why were we trying to change our ways and values? Or was there some hidden agenda underlying their plans. Emily certainly thought so.

Our world was becoming divided in a way that was even beginning to scare me a tiny bit. They called it political correctness but it was transforming into 'them and us'.

It had invaded our way of life to the degree that one had to be careful what came out of their mouth in public. It was causing a divide between people who'd once been friends. Groups of friends would often spend their time exposing one another's deficiencies, size, shape, accents or anything that could encourage a laugh. Humans picked on each other – that's just what they did. With adults it was mostly in jest, completely harmless and the best way to get a cheap laugh in a now all-too-serious world.

We'd come up with things to pick on each other about. Bradley was teased for his chicken legs – a tall, well-built man with skinny legs. Not that we often saw him wearing shorts, but once was enough to start the teasing. Muscular Dean, with his excessive body hair and chiselled, cave-man type features was referred to as King Kong.

Simone and I were constantly reminded how well we embodied the dumb blonde character for which there seemed to be no comeback, and we continually ribbed Jackie about the potential weight we predicted she would gain courtesy of her Italian heritage. Emily just seemed to embody mean; her straightforward honesty and lack of empathy for others led to her being referred to as the Ice Queen, Maleficent or any other evil character that turned up over time.

None of us had the pleasure of using the racism card because we weren't part of any recognised minority group, although we girls probably should have given it a try. I'm fairly sure we were often a little offended by the names directed at us like gorilla and dumb blonde. We got over it and enjoyed it for the joke it was, but now that there was money to be made through the courts from some harmless fun, it was safer to avoid anyone too different from you. That ribbing was just our group and I knew for a fact that it happened everywhere as it went on at work too. People always picked on each other to some degree and for this very reason it had become too dangerous to hang around someone of a different race, sexual orientation, or religion, as you knew there was no chance of not offending them. Now it could cost you, so it just wasn't worth taking the risk.

Emily found it ludicrous that so many in Western society spent so much energy telling its citizens that they were a bunch of racist losers. Seriously, she explained that their proof was incredibly thin, with multicoloured sporting heroes and entertainers, adored by the masses; where leaders with dark skin or different religions or sexual orientations were elected to represent us. If the West was so ignorant, how could this have happened? We never judged people by anything but their personality and behaviour, so why were we being criticised for a warped viewpoint we didn't actually have?

Western society was, as a general rule, incredibly open and tolerant to those of a different race or culture, and it drove Emily insane to be told otherwise. Actually it annoyed us all to be treated with such unwarranted contempt. Being told we could no longer apply for certain jobs because they needed people of a certain minority to keep their imposed quota. Now we all had to endure a whole new form of enforced racism that guaranteed separation and bad feelings to those that weren't exactly the same.

I remember originally trying to calm Emily every time a new law to discourage us from racist behaviour was suggested and generally put into practice. I'd try to explain to her how their heart was in the right place and what bad could come out of laws to protect people from bad behaviour. She knew and again proved me wrong.

The funny part about the new extreme views of the politically correct was the fact that the ones shoving their ideas down everyone's throats were often the biggest bullies of them all. They would have huge Twitter and Facebook campaigns against anyone that had the courage to question their ideas. Their disdain for people who didn't agree with their every word was obvious by the way they would crucify the disbeliever, be it a politician, reporter or anyone willing to speak against them. They would seriously manage to get away with treating people so badly that many actually lost their careers because of them. These were supposed to be the feel good, everybody is equal, no need to offend crusaders. Yet they were more dangerous than any evil they were supposedly trying to save the world from. A gigantic bunch of hypocrites that no-one seemed to notice or call out, except Emily of course, and she was the only reason I ever noticed the divisive behaviour they could get away with.

Unfortunately, Emily's problems went from bad to astronomically worse as Justin's need to destroy her life escalated. He began syphoning money from her accounts. Not large amounts: just enough to remind her that he had this power over her. If he had done the same to my account, I probably wouldn't have been any the wiser. We all knew it was Justin, but he was always a step ahead of the detectives trying to trip him up. With cybercrime at an all-time high, one would have hoped that law enforcement had found the tools to deal with it, but it wasn't the case.

The average person wanting to join the force was more the hands-on type; computer nerds could make much more money elsewhere. It's not that the police didn't try to help. They were just missing the tools to catch this new form of criminal, especially when there were now so many more of them. Justin was just a tiny fish in what was becoming an ocean of hackers. With every new strategy the police would initiate, the hackers would have it made obsolete by the next morning. I was beginning to fear anyone I met who claimed to be working in IT.

Jackie and Dean suggested that Emily find someone that Justin didn't know to stay with. Luckily enough she had an old friend of the family. She didn't see him often, and Justin had no knowledge of him at all. Bill was more than happy to help her out. He thought that it would be great to have company as his wife of many years had recently died, and someone young in the house might brighten it up a little. His house was modest and lacking the luxuries of her new-build apartment but it seemed safe, and at least there were two bathrooms and a carport to hide away her car.

My only visit to her had to be made with caution. Luckily her new room was incredibly large and able to accommodate the many amazing objects that she had collected from her travels. I'd never realised how many strange things she had accumulated but, now, being crammed into one room with her treasures, I found a new appreciation of her adventurous life. Photos of pyramids, majestic waterfalls, every imaginable animal, artefacts from countries too hard to find on a map – it was amazing and yet so very sad that she now had to hide away with them in a place she had only visited once before.

Emily's wage and savings were transferred straight into an account in Bill's name, and with tap and go, there was no need for her to sign. Handy given the account name – she really didn't look like a Bill. Emily had saved a lot, so it was very fortunate that she could trust Bill. I found the whole thing a little depressing, as even though my parents were very social, I seriously couldn't think of one family friend that would do the same for me.

I was actually jealous of my friend for having someone to help her out. How selfish those stupid inner thoughts can be sometimes. That's why they should never leave the sanctuary of your head. My friend was in deep trouble yet I could still find some way to feel that she was better off than me. I wondered if everyone did that, then I remembered Simone's nasty comments about one of Emily's holiday destinations. When the flight was delayed because of a volcanic eruption and Emily was stuck in the airport for two days, all Simone could say was, "Suffer! I hope she's stranded there for a week." So maybe we did all have that unwarranted jealousy of others, but at least I never told anyone about mine.

Emily worked for a large restaurant chain with many staff so it was hopefully going to take Justin a long time to work out where her money was going. As everything was done online, eventually he was going to be able to join the dots and work it out. The fact that she actually managed the restaurant made it even harder to hide as her wage was well above the others, so even though the chain tried to wangle her pay in strange inventive ways, we all knew that her reprieve from Justin was very limited.

Although very worried and stressed for Emily's safety, there wasn't a great deal I could do to help her. At least that was my excuse for getting on with my own life as it was finally looking up.

A magnificent male specimen made his way into the building and walked towards me. His scruffy blonde hair, oil-covered jeans and slightly ripped t-shirt excited me in a way I had never thought possible. This guy was hot and I did notice that I wasn't the only female paying him a little extra attention, but I was the receptionist so he had to come my way first.

He introduced himself as Michael Richly – a surname I would proudly take on. Usually confident at my desk, the strange chills running through my body rendered me useless. My responsible receptionist poker face was replaced by a childish grin while I uncontrollably giggled at Michael's not particularly amusing jokes. This was not the first man that I'd been attracted to, but he was the only one to make me weak at the knees, for lack of a better description. Then I recognised the name and realised his company was one of our larger clients. So why was such a wealthy man so incredibly different to Bradley – unpretentious, ridiculously attractive and a little too nice to me? With that thought my obsession with this gorgeous man calmed. I realised he was so out of my league there was no point wasting my thoughts on an unattainable fantasy, so I regained my composure, wiped the smile from my face and spoke to him as I did any other customer.

He seemed a little taken aback by my attitude swing then, unexpectedly, asked me out on a date. Just as I began slipping back towards being the blithering idiot, I managed to contain myself and agreed to go out with him. I had decided that my hard-to-get behaviour was probably the reason he'd asked me out, but I didn't want to go overboard and miss out completely. He'd just found himself an easy one-night stand was my only explanation for his behaviour but I could live with that. One night with the man of my dreams was a much better option than a night of re-runs on television.

Michael had arrived to pick me up half an hour earlier than planned so I was going on my dream date thirty minutes less attractive than I would have liked. It didn't matter because I was taking this whole experience as some sick joke he must have been playing on a less-than-desirable female just to bring up the number of women he'd conquered. I've seen a lot of college movies and he seemed too perfect to be true. I had never felt that I was out of anyone's league before, but I was glad that I did because it caused me to behave more honestly than I ever had before. I answered every question with complete candour and asked whatever inappropriate question entered my mind, like how he could run such a large mechanical business with over twenty employees at just twenty-eight.

It was a fairly blunt question for a first date, but one that was answered in more detail than I had expected. It seemed it was his family's business where he had begun working as a child. He had become a qualified mechanic before he'd reached eighteen, which was fortunate, because when he was twenty-two his parents died unexpectedly in a car accident. It was left to Michael to take charge of the business and continue his father's legacy.

His older sisters had their own lives and were more than happy for him to have the business, which was handy as it was already stated in their parents' will. Michael loved his work and his employees so he was more than prepared to make sure he lived up to his father's expectations.

We had the most amazing night, talking for hours and hours about our pasts and our dreams for the future. If he was just putting on a front to get laid, his brilliant acting skills were being completely wasted. I always intended to sleep with him, and I did.

Turned out that my date wasn't some college-type practical joke. Michael really liked me. We became almost inseparable. I had found myself the perfect man and, to be honest, it was more magical than I could have ever imagined. I now understood those soppy love stories I'd previously considered absolute crap. That falling in love thing was true and I really had trouble wiping the smile from my face, which was really not cool around Emily. She never really seemed to mind. I'm sure that she would have told me if she did.

But she never had the chance to relax for very long. She knew Justin was stalking her and it was only a matter of time until he worked out where she was hiding all of her money. She was now preparing to leave the country and change her name. Luckily the restaurant chain she worked for had restaurants in many cities throughout the world and they were more than happy to help her relocate. I didn't want her to leave but I was so wrapped up in my new life with Michael I sort of encouraged her new idea.

She was bringing sadness into my new perfect world. I felt terrible because I had never understood the way many people changed when they met a new love, and after watching Simone, I promised it would never happen to me. I was going to follow Emily's example. She changed nothing to accommodate her boyfriends, not even delaying one of her flights for a day to visit one in hospital after he broke his leg. But I did change.

From nowhere, Michael had shot up to the top of my list over anything or anyone. It was all about him – nothing else mattered. Against my better judgment I was following Simone's example. I was just lucky my man was not the proverbial wanker hers was. That's why I momentarily felt so bad for Emily. I knew that without Michael around I would have been spending my time with her trying to sort out her problems. She had to have noticed it too. Then I realised I didn't need to feel sorry for her because the last thing she wanted was my useless pity, annoying her daily. Wasting her time with useless ideas and, much worse, constantly letting her know how bad I felt for her was something she would not tolerate.

She always seemed so much more excited to see me with Michael and encouraged me to call him when I was with her. It sometimes seemed that Emily was even happier about my relationship than I was. She loved Michael because he was keeping me occupied, like a puppy amused with a bone, so its owner could quickly escape to go off and do important things. I was the dog and it was a bit rude of her but probably a fair call. I even started thinking that maybe she had just hired Michael to keep me busy and, if it was true, I didn't really care because it was nicely working for both of us.

Her apartment sold, leaving her a dismal profit of five hundred dollars after repaying the loan. It should have been her greatest investment but not owning it long and having to sell in such a hurry completely ruined her long-term goal. When she was just days away from beginning her new life, I received a phone call from her work – she hadn't shown up. She wasn't answering her phone and she had never missed a shift at work, even turning up with a broken collarbone straight after leaving the hospital.

Bill had told them that she had wanted to spend one last night in her apartment so he hadn't seen her either. He had no idea how unusual it was for her to not show up at work, and the restaurant didn't feel the need to worry him. They had no problem worrying me. My easy-going boss was more than happy for me to take time off and check up on my friend. She was so close to leaving. Maybe she'd tried something different like a big night out and was sleeping off a hangover, I thought. It was highly unlikely – she really didn't drink much alcohol and would usually have invited me.

I needed to think optimistic thoughts as this was so completely out of character for Emily and, to be honest, I was a little worried about what I was going to find. I had never been so annoyed by my employer's insistence on me taking time off to look for my friend. Why couldn't he make me stay at work, then I could have made Jackie or Dean look for her, but no, he had to be Mr Supportive. I never really forgave him.

000-05-000

I ARRIVED AT EMILY'S apartment and began knocking heavily on the dead-bolted front door. To my horror, it shot open. I yelled her name but there was no answer. As I cautiously walked down the long hall way to the bedroom, the uneasy feeling of being trapped in a B-grade horror movie completely consumed me. The relief of seeing her lying in the bed was overwhelming. I was so excited my first theory was correct – Emily was going to wake up with one mighty headache. With a huge grin I raced over to shake her then came to an abrupt halt when I noticed her lifeless eyes wide open.

I knew she was dead, and apart from the blood-curdling scream I let out, I froze. An elderly neighbour had heard my shriek, raced into the room, grabbed the phone from my hand and rang for an ambulance before checking on Emily.

"I'm sorry, I think she's been gone a while," he said to me. "And by the marks on her neck, I think he strangled her." As my body began to heat up in anger, defrosting my ice-like state, I managed to wipe the escaping vomit from my lips. We both immediately knew that it was Justin.

"How did he know she was here?" I questioned the neighbour. He shook his head in despair. He had no idea, he had heard nothing, and he didn't even realise that she had come back. There was no sign of a struggle and, knowing Emily, I had no doubt that she would have fought back. He obviously had plenty of time to tidy up and put her neatly into bed, with barely a wrinkle in the bedcover. Seriously, he murdered my friend then took the time to tidy up. What type of psycho does that?

For all the bad behaviour he had been displaying, there had still been no real sign, to me at least, that he could have become a killer. Ruining her life was one thing, but actually taking it away really didn't make any sense to me. How could he possibly murder the person that he supposedly had to have back? Spending every waking minute to find a way to make her return to him, then making damn sure she never could. He was not only crazy – he was obviously incredibly stupid as well.

As the room filled up with police and ambulance officers, the neighbour and I continually repeated Justin's name to them. We knew it was him and we intended to make sure that they did too.

Through all the commotion I recognised my phone's distinctive ring and I would have ignored it had it not shown Michael's name. He was phoning me to tell Emily he thought Justin might have worked out the account her wage was going into. One of Michael's employees happened to be a computer whiz and he had been busy trying to hack into Justin's computer to help us try and turn the tables on him.

Last night he had succeeded, but he realised that Justin had finally located Emily. Her last few hours were there on Justin's computer – from the servo close to her home where she had stocked up on chips and chocolate, to the movie that she rented through her television provider. The last one was her fatal mistake! Unfortunately, Michael's employee didn't realise the significance of this information, but then again, I'm not sure any of us did. We knew Justin was a problem; we had no idea he was killer. As I listened, staring at the dead body of my friend, my anger reached a point I could never have conceived.

"Yeah, thanks for that. But tell your friend, it's a bit fucking late. She's dead!" I threw the phone across the room, hurtling it like a missile into Emily's chest of drawers. It didn't explode into tiny pieces like I had planned but it seemed that the overcrowded room had noticed my little tantrum. One of the detectives picked up the phone and explained the situation to Michael in a more subtle way than I had.

The neighbour and I were eventually shuffled out of the room and taken out of the unit. As I walked through the door in a state of blind confusion, there was Michael, waiting right outside. I really wanted to hit him or just belt anyone, but he grabbed me so tightly I just fell into his arms and collapsed like a limp rag. The pent-up tears ran down my cheeks, possibly ruining his ugly, suede jacket I'd never liked anyway. I had wanted to take my aggression out on someone but the jacket would do for now while I could still take comfort in Michael's protective embrace.

Just as April's murder had been reported as a hitchhiker killing without any of the background story, the news coverage of Emily's death was as a domestic dispute, without any mention of the stalking or the events that led up to it. I rang the television stations and the papers, begging them to publish the whole truth, but they felt that there was no need to report on the fact that he had found access to her accounts and could trace her every move. Circulating it all over Facebook, Twitter and YouTube led to nothing again. I found that after posting something, it disappeared within a few hours.

Social media couldn't stop terrorists sending out recruitment material but they could delete my words in record time. It was incredibly frustrating, especially the fact that no-one else cared. Michael pretended to but he did nothing to help. I felt the need to reveal Emily's story to the world and it wouldn't listen. Even my friends, who were supposedly hers too, did nothing. They just kept telling me that it wasn't going to bring her back so why bother trying. After the effort we had all put into exposing April's case to no avail, I knew that they were right. It seemed that April and Emily had both died in ways that were not worth reporting to the public, who possibly didn't care because they were more interested in athlete's and celebrities' lives.

I'm not convinced it was their choice but there seemed to be a lot more irrelevant rubbish taking up the mediums that once declared to be reporters of news. I really missed my friend and I hated that the rest of the world couldn't even pretend to grieve with me, or at least be warned of the dangers this new cyber world could bring upon them.

Justin was immediately arrested. He was actually waiting for the police and confessed when they arrived. I was unable to share Emily's story but no-one was going to stop me finding out what turned a once decent guy into a killer. Unfortunately my first, and hopefully last, prison visit was not as enlightening as I'd envisioned. I was hoping for the phone conversation interview that I had seen so many times on television but, no, I had to actually sit in a room with Justin and other prisoners with their visitors. It reminded me of a preschool, filled with plastic tables and chairs, with toys in the corner for the poor little children dragged into see their criminal fathers. It was only the presence of armed guards and the heavily tattooed men that quickly wiped the original kiddyland image from my mind.

If I'd been pre-warned I would have to physically face Justin, I might have at least found away to bring in a weapon and finish him off. Probably not, but it was a fun thought for a minute. Luckily for me Justin looked like the bedraggled mess of a man I was hoping for. The chunks of flesh missing from his cheeks needed no explanation but she had caused so much damage to his manhood he could barely walk, or take a seat, it would have been excruciating to watch anyone else in his predicament. He pleaded for forgiveness I refused to give, explaining how much he loved and had to have Emily, but when she cut him off to the point he knew she was not returning, he just lost control.

"You do realise that she's dead because of you!" I snapped at him, still trying to understand what he expected to gain from killing her. "You will never ever see her again, which was supposedly what you wanted – to see her!"

"She was never going to be mine again," he replied sulkily.

"Not now she's dead, you idiot. If you cared about her at all, you wouldn't have done that. You're right. I doubt she would have ever returned to you, but stranger things have happened. Had you been ridiculously nice and done amazing things to beg her forgiveness, who knows what could have been. We won't now because you killed her, you asshole. I hope somehow she haunts you for the rest of your life." His snivelling façade disappeared as his true evil began to surface, scaring me a little until I noticed the guard watching closely as he angrily described the injuries that Emily had caused to his manhood.

I saw the anger that must have confronted Emily as Justin's eyes seemed to turn a shark-like shade of black, but unlike her, I was safe. Surrounded by heavily armed protection, I rose from my seat, making sure to be completely out of his arms' reach, I conjured up my inner Emily moment with what I hoped to be a parting statement that might somehow make his imprisonment a little more uncomfortable.

"Suffer, you dumb prick," I said quietly. Then with plenty of volume so all the other inmates could hear, "You must be so happy to be finally making your transition into a woman and losing that annoying penis. You're about to become the cock-less fairy you've always dreamed of." He flung himself across the table towards me, but security had him down in a second, and after a light reprimand from one of the guards, I got to leave with a smile.

Time passed and although not forgotten, Emily's memory was becoming very distant. My life with Michael was heading in an exciting direction. I'd found my perfect match and was enjoying every minute of it. Unfortunately the world around us seemed to be heading in a stranger direction, changing at a weirdly rapid pace that scared me.

Simone received the mark on her hand as Bradley had promised that she would be one of the first. It actually came in very handy for me because she was constantly shouting me things. Every time I went out with her I would be scratching around my purse to find a card that might have money left on it. Simone being impatient at the checkout would just shove her hand under the scanner and cover me.

I knew she had a joint account with Bradley so I often bought things I knew I couldn't really afford. It was Bradley's shout so I felt no guilt at all. You're probably sensing that I'm not of great character, and you'd be right, but everyone has some bad traits and I don't think mine were that detrimental to anyone except Bradley who wouldn't have noticed anyway.

I was fast becoming one of the very few people carrying cards around. It was all Emily's fault. Her reaction to Bradley receiving the mark was deeply etched into my mind. Had she said nothing, I would have barcoded myself the second I had the chance – never having to worry about losing another card or having to scratch around to find one that worked because they would all be deeply etched into my hand. I didn't know how they could tell which account they were using and I never did think to ask. I couldn't keep track of my money with cards so what would be the difference.

What I found really adorable was the fact that Michael was happy to go along with my strange behaviour and avoid the mark as well. We began noticing the difference when we shopped, as people would become very annoyed with us wasting precious seconds while we took a piece of plastic from our wallet. Now I understood how those last cash users must have felt, except Emily who had been more than happy to make others wait. People really looked annoyed at us, like they had something better to be doing. Even the cashiers behaved like we were wasting their time – not that there were many of them left to upset. It was pretty well all self-serve.

The occasional place would have a manned checkout to help out the elderly and anyone else willing to wait a really long time to have their bags packed more professionally. If you were under eighty, others would look down on you for standing in that line.

Banks too had become a thing of the past as everything was now done online, from moving your money around, to applying for a loan. Emily had warned us all before. She had refused to use the ATM back in the days of cash. We would have to stand in line waiting for her to take out her weekly wage or at least part of it in cash. I would just cringe when I noticed one of the employees making their way through the line, trying to take customers out so they could teach them how to use the machine rather than have to wait in line. It happened every single time I was there and Emily was always prepared to tell them why she didn't want to.

"You do realise that you are actually encouraging the demise of your own job." Emily would love to point out to the staff member.

They would usually reply with the standard, "No, I'm not. This is just for your convenience."

"No, it's purely to avoid paying wages and when you're unemployed, you can just remember that I told you so," Emily would end with a smug look upon her face. So the whole often-repeated incident would just send an embarrassed shiver up my spine, making me hope that the staff never made it to her. Unfortunately most times they did.

As I had tried to explain to Emily, it was their job to encourage her to use the ATM, and even if they knew it was causing future job losses, there wasn't anything they could do about it. She had agreed with me completely but, as was often the case, all the customers in the same line heard her little rant and the majority of them declined to use the machine too so I was never going to be able to stop her.

Of course again she had been right. Very quickly the full-service banks started disappearing and turning into human-free rooms full of ATMs. Then with no cash, there was nothing. Everything was now online and that was it. It was as easy as writing your name. Once the computer had your details, everything about you came up, loan accepted or, in my case, probably loan denied. No human loan officer to plead your case to, no personal touch. They knew everything you spent, every cent, and of course they charged you for that two minutes on the internet like they charged you for pretty well everything you did, and you could do nothing to stop them.

The banks no longer needed to waste their money on staffed buildings. Of course it was all done for our convenience, they said, but their enormous profits proved otherwise. They now only had a few buildings full of computers and a few technicians to watch over them. They still kept their hierarchy, CEOs and a few dozen people just to make sure everything was running as it should, but customer service was gone. There was still phone access, but like everything to avoid high wages, it was all offshore and the phone operators didn't even seem to bother learning much English any more. Perhaps it was set up that way to make it so hard people just gave up. Like public transport, airports, post offices and so many other things that had once employed thousands, we were becoming completely reliant on computers even though their dependability really hadn't improved.

Computer criminals were outnumbering drug dealers and actually causing a lot more grief to the growing number of victims. Identity theft was becoming as common as the cold, lending support to the campaign to mark everyone with their own personal barcode. It may have stopped identity theft for a moment but it certainly had no effect on the criminals' ability to wipe their bank accounts. As you walked down the street, a criminal could secretly scan your hand, giving them full access to your finances and any other information about you that they wanted. They'd been doing it to cards and phones for a long time, but it now seemed the hand was even easier. People actually had to be careful when shopping as their hands could now get swiped accidently by just waving them near a scanner. This was never reported but I had heard people complain at work.

Michael and I were lucky in our employment for the moment, both working in the motoring industry, where cars and trucks continued to break down for him to fix and for me to answer the phone for whatever automobile parts they were that we sold. Michael tried to explain what it was that my company sold but I continually reminded him that I didn't need to know so I was never going to listen.

On one of our last dinner nights out with Simone, Bradley, Dean and Jackie, we were given the news that Michael and I were the only remaining couple without the barcode in our arms. Jackie said that she really didn't have any choice – it was just getting too hard to shop otherwise. She was correct. As fewer and fewer shops were taking cards, the choice was disappearing. It was continually being sold as the most secure option for our protection. I remembered Emily reminding us how the same stunt was pulled when they disposed of cash. They originally charged more for you to access your cash, basically forcing you into the cheaper option of using cards or phones. It was the safer, more convenient choice until it was the only option, which proved not to be that safe and a lot more expensive. Originally it was cheaper to pay bills with cards or direct debit, then large companies went further and gave discounts to have direct access to your accounts. The discount disappeared when the choice no longer existed. Cheque books became obsolete leaving people completely reliant on those bank statements they had to access online – now their only real record of the whereabouts of their money.

With no other proof but the banks' records, in time people were really losing track of their finances. I thought it was just me but it seemed there were many, especially with all of the new little charges that kept turning up. Paying your bills online occasionally caused a problem for those of us that weren't computer literate.

I once accidently pressed an extra zero on a water usage payment that took me three months to get back. The water provider's answer to my problem was to consider myself lucky that I would be in credit for a long time, ignoring the fact that without them replacing my money I would just starve to death and therefore never use their expensive prepaid water. It was actually my parents who fought to get them to return my money because they were the ones that had to cover the extra money I couldn't afford to be without. The wonderful advantages of being an only child – I had cheap rent and no siblings to point out my shortcomings to my parents.

I began feeling a little more relieved about Emily's passing as I really don't know how she would have handled this new world with her good friends all succumbing to the mark that had horrified her. I finally decided to read this Book of Revelation. I possibly should have read the whole Bible for a better understanding but it was a really big book, so Revelation should have covered it. I was lucky that Michael had a copy of the Bible because when I tried to look it up online, the Revelation part of it was missing, putting an interesting twist on this whole saga. Even after paying to download a copy, the same part I wanted was missing, causing me to become very suspicious of its contents.

Sitting on the couch with a fresh cup of coffee I was a little excited and scared about understanding why I had been avoiding this mark after Emily's warning. Naturally, I didn't understand a thing, except the passage that Emily had referred to about the mark containing the number of the beast – the one part that could not be construed to mean anything other than what it said. No-one would be able to buy or sell without it, and only those without the mark would enter heaven after suffering on Earth for a while. Those with the mark, although in a better position on Earth, would eventually be destined to suffer for eternity in hell.

I was beginning to share Emily's fear. I can honestly say that I never came across any of the dragon beasts with ten horns and seven heads that featured in the story, but I assume you were supposed to take that figuratively. The mark however was proving to be an extremely obvious entity, substantiating the Bible preachings. What really confused me was the fact that this was one of the best-selling books in the world. Did nobody read it? I'm not a religious person – the Immaculate Conception and parting the Red Sea seemed way to unrealistic for me to ever go down that path. I was still always happy to celebrate Christmas and Easter regardless.

With that many sales, someone had to have read it, so why would the world ever risk going down this path in the first place? What were they thinking? It had been written hundreds of years ago, so it's not as if we didn't have the time to contemplate the possible risk it involved. Perhaps it was like the book and film *Jurassic Park*, one of my all-time favourites. The point of the story was that humans and dinosaurs were separated for a very good reason, yet scientists continued to try to find ways to bring them back. Perhaps it's just that reckless human response many of us have imbedded in our nature, like pressing the button that says don't touch. Let's be honest, the majority of us have done it at least once, although setting off an alarm seemed a little less serious.

I did wish I hadn't read it, especially knowing that somehow the relevant passages had been wiped from the web entirely. Why would that have happened unless someone was trying to hide something they didn't want us to know? It would never have become that successful as there were already so many copies printed, but I suppose if you weren't looking for Revelation you'd be none the wiser that it was gone, alleviating the need to search for a hard copy. Someone somewhere no longer wanted people to read it, and that fact alone made the whole thing more terrifying. The next day I visited Emily's gravesite to abuse her.

Our last dinner with friends was a very uncomfortable night with Bradley telling us how behind the times we were for not having a barcode on our hand. I felt most sorry for Michael because it was my fault that he was in this position as an unmarked outcast. I had a gorgeous man actually going along with my reckless behaviour, and we had agreed not to tell them what we had read, not because they would think we were mad, but to protect them from the fact that their choice might cause them all irreparable damage. Or at least scare the crap out of them. But their persistent bantering became too much for me.

"Because of Emily," I blurted out.

"You seriously believed that rubbish she was saying that night?" said Jackie. "She was stressed out by Justin."

"And rightly so!" added Simone.

"Yeah, well I read it," I replied. "I don't suggest that you guys do the same."

"What are we all going to burn in hell?" asked Bradley belligerently.

"That's what it says," replied Michael.

I think they all read Revelation when they returned home because they never really talked to me again. What I should have explained to them, and the other reason that I still hadn't taken the mark, was the fact that all of Emily's rantings were becoming reality. With no cash we were all completely at the mercy of our basically staffless banks and governments that could track our every move. They could and they did charge us whatever they liked, and we were now powerless to fight them. The smaller banks had all disappeared, leaving no real competition, so we couldn't even play the I'll-take-my-money-elsewhere card – there was nowhere to take it. One put up their interest rate on loans; the next day the others followed. It should have been no surprise as they had always behaved that way, but now we really had nowhere else to go. Making interest on our money had all but disappeared because they didn't need to offer incentives to bank with them. There was no other money, no other choice.

We truly had nowhere else to go. Every cent we made was now fully controlled by the institutions that no longer needed to offer incentives, so they didn't. The share market was our only option to try to make some interest but it was becoming so turbulent that the risks were just way too high for those of us who couldn't afford to lose our hard-earned money. There were extremely high suicide rates for investors. Emily had warned us all over and over again but we didn't listen.

What annoyed me the most about this new world was the fact that it should have been the greatest time of my life. I had found the most perfect, wonderful, gorgeous man I could ever have dreamed of, and life was becoming too hard to enjoy it. Even from the safety of my apartment where Michael and I spent every romantic night together, a television commercial or the news would remind us of the scariness waiting outside. The media was starting to put down those of us without the mark. Current affair programs and talk shows would refer to us as backward religious freaks who couldn't be trusted. It had started by mocking us as being behind the times.

"I was in the supermarket the other day," began one of those beautifully dressed, holier-than-thou chat show hosts. "And I was stuck behind someone fiddling through their handbag trying to find their card." The other hosts shook their heads in annoyed agreement as if it was something that they had all had to suffer before. "What is wrong with these people?" she continued, with the others nodding in agreement. "Don't they know that my time is valuable, and I really shouldn't have to wait around for their odd beliefs."

Seriously she lost two minutes tops, but no, the panel were all happily in agreement with her complaint, as were those twittering their annoying comments along the screen. That's how it began mildly, not ridiculously offensive but acceptable gripes. It really didn't stay that way for long.

000-06-000

MY RELATIONSHIP WITH MICHAEL was becoming incredibly serious when he arrived at my apartment for a long weekend of locked-away-from-the-rest-of-the-world sex.

"Come, we are going for a drive," he said with a scary grin on his face.

"Ok," I agreed, a little sceptical of this excitement I had never seen him display before. No matter how much I pestered him, like a small child nagging their parents in the car "Are we there yet?", he would not give away where he was taking me. I even asked that actual question a few times. I assumed we were heading for town as he drove along the road I used to commute daily to work.

"I'd love to live here," I exclaimed with passion as we drove along the beautiful stretch of tree-lined homes I had always dreamed of. Then he pulled into the driveway of one of them, not the smaller pretty ones, but one of the awesome, long and treed ones.

"So you know rich people!" I exclaimed, thinking we were there to meet one of his rich friends.

With his ridiculous grin still overtaking his face, he coaxed me to the front door, knelt down on one knee and pulled a magnificent ring and a set of keys from his pocket.

"Marry me," he said, "and all this could be yours." I would have said yes if he'd asked me that question overlooking a tent with a plastic key ring.

In awe and shock I was led into the sparsely furnished mansion with its grand staircase and 'Gone with the Wind' style extravagance.

"We need to go furniture shopping," he said.

"I haven't said yes," I reminded him, still deeply shocked that anything like this could actually happen to anyone, especially me.

"But you will," he replied with confidence. He should not have said that because now he'd left me no other choice but to drag out that yes, and drag I did. It didn't really help that he was so excited and he knew I would marry him regardless of giving him the answer. I was taken around the spectacular manor in absolute awe of its beauty and grandeur.

"Awful big house to clean," I stated, still not believing the situation I was now in. "It wasn't for sale. I drive past it everyday. I would have noticed the sign."

"It's been partly mine for years," said Michael calmly. "It was my family home. I just sold my apartment and paid out my sisters' share of the property. They kindly gave me a good price."

"So this is for real? It's not some evil cruel prank you're playing on me?" I asked, and then blurted out, "I would have married you without the house," ruining my plan to drag out the suspense.

"I know," he replied smugly.

My life was now perfect – the man and house of my dreams. There had to be a catch but the only one I could think of was my car. I was going to have to upgrade because it would be way too embarrassing having that piece of junk entering such a driveway.

I moved in with my beloved within a week of being invited. It was amazing flittering around my mansion like Scarlett O'Hara. The world was all mine, but no matter how many times I phoned my friends they ignored my invitations to visit. I now had the bragging rights of a movie star but no-one to impress. Even my parents ignored my constant requests to see my exciting new life. You would think that they would be ridiculously happy for me, and if not for me, themselves as they could now rent out their flat for real money and would no longer have to financially bail me out. That was now Michael's problem.

It's not that my parents and friends didn't talk to me. They answered my calls and were friendly enough but short and sweet and always full of excuses of why they couldn't see me. It was just really odd; they had a barcode on their hand and I didn't. I felt like a leper. I wasn't infectious but I was certainly treated like someone that was. My work colleagues had no idea that I was missing the mark because it wasn't visible, then all of a sudden it was.

As the world we knew began falling apart at the seams, even the wealthy were starting to notice significant changes in their lives. With now mass unemployment in the low to middle income bracket there was a huge drop in spending.

Against Emily's wishes we had all accepted the lack of customer service and now it was pretty much all gone. Big business had destroyed its competition; little shops were a thing of the past. Supermarket generic brands filled the aisles replacing our old favourites and putting more people out of work. Of course, the generic brands were no longer cheap because they didn't need to be – we had no other choice. We self-served now with computers, buying everything else online and having it delivered by drones. Technology had given us so many wonderful things but there were now few of us who could afford it.

It turned out that if you wipe out the incomes of so many, a ripple effect ensures that you soon wipe the incomes of all. No point having great things to sell if there is no-one left to buy them. Even the great unflappable Bradley began to notice as the banks shed their high flyers too. He hadn't lost his job but he was under a lot of pressure to keep it. Simone was happily unemployed – the clothing store she worked for now completely online. She'd seen it coming but with Bradley supporting her it didn't matter. Jackie and Dean were surviving, as people still needed their hair done and their clients were loyal but even they were suffering. They had to lower their prices to compete with the multinational cheap-cuts chain down the road. The end was coming soon and they knew it.

All of a sudden farming was becoming the new safe industry to get involved in. People still needed to eat but you now needed a degree in physics to be a fruit picker, ruling my chances out to have that as a fall back. As times had turned tense, people worried about their future or lack of it;the discussion of those marked and those not intensified.

As those marked outnumbered, or at least included the most powerful people, it was decided that it would be a great idea to light up those barcodes. They had the technology and even if it was not a popular decision, they went ahead and did it anyway. There was now no real way of hiding the fact that you hadn't joined the masses.

I found it ironic that in the Holocaust it was those that had been marked who were singled out to suffer – this time it was to be the other way around. Could the Jewish community ever have imagined the horror of what was to befall them? Did they see the early warning signs? Could they have had any idea of what was to come? How did once-normal human beings ever let this happen?

The idea of eradicating an entire race of human beings was not just considered – it was implemented. How could this ever have eventuated? How could the masses have been swayed to follow one man's insane vision. So what went wrong? How did a country become a place where some, not all that much different, were no longer considered anything but disposable?

Most serial killers know that what they are doing is wrong but they have the twisted outlook that they don't care. How could a whole society go down that same path? What could have possessed them to commit these atrocities, or have knowledge of what was happening and do nothing to stop it? It seemed too unbelievable to imagine yet it did happen and so very many lost their lives for nothing.

I remembered part of a saying – the only way for evil to prosper is for good men to do nothing. I thought because we were more civilised now and with the internet, the good people could not fail to notice what was happening. We had to hope that unlike in the past, there would be many more good men or women to fight for what was right and just. I'm sure that they were out there. It just would have been nice to hear them. They'd turn up, I thought, if things ever started turning bad, because the world was smarter now and it had learnt by its past disasters. My grandmother always told me that I was entitled to make mistakes as long I didn't repeat them, so I now prayed that the world was going to heed her advice.

Walking outside, everywhere you turned hands shone with a translucent green tattoo as if they'd all escaped from a nightclub. It looked ridiculous but as there were more of them, it was those of us without it who felt embarrassed. Wearing gloves only brought attention to the fact that you didn't have the mark. Times had begun turning a lot harder with staggering prices for common necessities like electricity, as we basically depended on the sun shining or the wind blowing to save us all from the supposed horrors of the world prematurely warming– a better option than the turmoil we were about to embark on, at least we could have all been suffering with a good tan.

You would have thought that these natural energy sources would have been a cheaper option but it didn't turn out that way. Like our hideously expensive water that fell from the sky, it had to be contained and distributed to our properties. To be charged for that was fair but such excessive prices were not. We had already had to pay to install solar panels at no cost to the government, yet now they charged us for the pleasure of catching and containing it. They had added meters to our roof top panels and charged us for how much sunlight we collected. I'm not even sure that they had the technology to do this but it wasn't relevant because we would be charged regardless. It was not only expensive, but incredibly unreliable – a huge problem for a world now completely reliant on power. Nuclear power was a goner too as it was now considered too dangerous even though it had been used safely for years.

With competition now all but extinguished, everything cost more, and with less of us employed, people were becoming scared and started turning back to religion. This meant reading the Bible and wondering if they had made the right choice. Of course only those with a hard copy could have come across the crucial verses. Reading the Book of Revelation, even if one didn't believe a word of it, would have to have been scary for someone now stuck with a non-removable tattoo. They had to have noticed that the predictions in these dark passages were coming true. By accident or intent, we would probably never know, being branded with that mark seemed to support this.

Was the end near or were we just going to endure some new kind of normal? Probably the latter, as this religious stuff seemed to be full of suffering and sacrifice. Supposedly it was meant to represent forgiveness, but nowhere did it state that option was available to the marked. Forgiven for everything except that hand imprint. So if you believed the writings and you had the mark, you seemed to be pretty well screwed.

The fanatics walking city streets with placards warning all that they were destined for hell didn't really help. It was terrifying walking past these nutcases bellowing their aversion to the mark and reciting Bible passages from Revelation with such passion that they scared me. Prophets had been taking to the streets for many years but now they seemed so much more empowered and frightening. Once you could avoid and ignore them but not anymore. They were everywhere and so much more passionate. Then one day they were all gone;no-one ever explained the disappearance. I suppose no-one cared.

I had it all, the perfect boyfriend, a magnificent house. All my dreams had come true, plus some. Would I have noticed anything wrong with the world if I just got that stupid mark on my hand? I don't know and worse, I don't understand why I didn't. Having my hero Michael by my side, I didn't notice the changes as quickly as others but they were becoming more and more obvious. Originally, the people at work treated me the same, openly picking on my lack of glowing hand and calling me the Naked One, but it was done with a smile and a laugh. It didn't even bother me when they changed it to "Kojak", a bald lollypop-sucking detective from a seventies television series.

I never really understood how my lack of a marked hand could cause a comparison with a bald detective but it seemed harmless. But comments made in jest soon turned to offensive. Michael was an important customer of theirs, and they made it quite clear that he was the only reason I still had a job. I used to think these people liked me. If anything, I'd improved at my job. Now I knew what it was that my company sold:mufflers and all parts associated with the exhaust system. So why had they all turned on me? Michael had no problem at his work, possibly being the boss helped.

Not being a real news enthusiast, I decided it was time that changed and began reading newspapers trying to emulate my new namesake Kojak's detective skills. It was quite the eye-opener to see little stabs at those of us who hadn't conformed to receiving the mark. Columnists wrote as though we were somehow the reason for the decline in employment and the skyrocketing prices of all our essential services. As ridiculous as it sounded, the way it was written I almost believed it myself.

Their argument was that it was extremely costly to compensate for those of us who couldn't be scanned. We were causing immense problems, as we were supposedly no longer paying our way and costly to track down. We had become identified with the evil hackers, emptying the accounts of victims being scanned in the streets and losing their entire savings. All of a sudden we were the new cyber criminals, even though I very much doubted many unmarked people were even slightly computer literate. I knew that Michael and I weren't.

Having one's entire identity encrypted in their hand was proving riskier than the old dangers of keeping it on their mobile. People with the mark were continually being ripped off, while those of us still using a card were obviously a little harder to steal from. Instead of admitting that perhaps they had made a mistake with their new technology and returning to cash, or at least cards, they turned against those of us who were still resisting the change. I was becoming enemy number one and really beginning to notice it.

Common sense had disappeared. I think it was just easier to blame people who were different rather than admit they had caused the problem themselves, and that included me. Before Emily stopped me, I was more than happy to use the self-serve in the supermarket and transact everything online rather than waste my time entering a bank.

I never intended to write a letter – to be honest, I think that started to phase out with the invention of a telephone. I don't even recall my grandmother writing letters. People just found it quicker and easier to do everything via the internet. The old adage of nothing is free soon came to be as people were now also being charged for sending and receiving emails too. The once-free communication tool had now become the only way one could receive their bills, and with no other alternative, it now came with a fee. They didn't even bother with an excuse because they didn't need to explain; it was our only option.

It turned out that I wasn't the only one who had trouble keeping track of my finances once they became exclusively online. I'm sure Emily would have printed off every single transaction she ever made but most of us didn't so keeping track of our funds was causing many people a great deal of problems, especially now that it was becoming very hard to buy a printer. I assumed they were still around for legal documents and such things, but they were now impossible to find for the rest of us. The explanation for their departure was lack of sales, like the CD and faxes before them. No-one bothered to print hard copies anymore – all information was now stored on computers, tablets or phones. So everything lived in cyberspace, once unimportant to me, but for someone like Emily, it would have been horrendous not having that piece of paper to refer to.

If your computer crashed, as they always did, and you didn't back up everything, and most people didn't, your proof of so many important things was now completely gone. They could attempt to employ someone to find all their records at an astronomical price that most couldn't afford or just reconcile themselves to no longer having any of their important records. Losing their identities before they'd even been robbed of them caused people no end of grief and wasted time reconstructing their records.

Those original guarantees by the banks that they would make-good computer theft because their systems were so safe were a thing of the past. Emily had warned us every time the banks advertised new technology to help us protect our own accounts. She would point out the dangers of them constantly finding ways to shift the onus onto the customer. She was correct and they now did exactly that. It was now your money and up to you to protect it even though they were the ones completely controlling it. Again, that was all now somehow the fault of those not succumbing to the mark because we were now making it harder for the banks to keep track of funds. Seriously? The banks controlled our money in the exact same manner but, as I said, that whole commonsense thing had completely disappeared from society. I was beginning to understand how good people could turn bad with a little coaxing. In tough times people became disheartened and unfortunately, the majority were more susceptible to brainwashing.

It cost hundreds of thousands of lives in Rwanda in what to the rest of us seemed unbelievable. Hutus, Tootsies – no, you're Rwandan. How can you really be suckered in to slaughtering one another? Emily had visited there many years after the bloodshed when men, women, children, even newborn babies had been slaughtered in their thousands by their neighbours. She told us how lovely the people had been to her and what a wonderful holiday it had been. She also mentioned the strange feelings she had when it dawned on her that perhaps her guide had once slaughtered people in cold blood. Not a question she asked but a possibility when she worked out his age. She found the whole idea chilling.

Cambodia was another strange 'Emily' destination, given the fact that they had also slaughtered so many of their own. It had not been as recent but she still knew the ridiculously friendly people that made her holiday awesome could have once been involved. Not only could people become pure evil, it seemed that they also had the ability to return back to decent human beings. I'm not sure what really scared me more, the fact that humans could become irrational psychotic killers or that they could so easily return to the way they had been previously. The Jekyll and Hyde syndrome, Emily used to call it.

She truly believed that we all had some inner beast lurking, ready to appear when the climate was conducive. A touch of fear stirred into resentment and self-pity made a neat little package to be sculptured into whatever the powers that be desired. So said Emily. I never really understood what she meant but as the world traveller, I just accepted her analogy as gospel. Given the fact she rated humans below aardvarks, I probably should not have relied on her theories. On the other hand I didn't have a better one so I would just hope that humans weren't inherently evil – a hope that was fast evaporating. Especially in light of the ongoing slaughter at the hands of religious extremists. It seemed like we'd learnt nothing.

I did however notice that every one of these horrendous moments in time had something scarily in common: the them and us divide. Opposing sides needed to exist for tensions to ever begin. I was possibly now on that weaker side of this new evolving division.

After a fairly nasty day at work of being completely ignored or spoken down to when my fellow-workers had to acknowledge me, I decided to take the plunge and visit my once best friend, Simone. I probably needed to visit Jackie and Dean first as I was desperate for a trim, but they had scissors so I felt it safer to test out Simone first.

When I entered Simone and Bradley's apartment – that not only looked like a page from a magazine but had actually been displayed in one – I no longer felt like the loser I had on previous visits. Yes, it was absolutely beautiful, but now I lived in a mansion with a magnificent garden and a ton of land. I had finally beaten them at their envious lifestyle game but, of course, they never visited so I could gloat silently. Who am I kidding? There would have been nothing silent about it – maybe that was the reason they all ignored me now.

The biggest-loser friend had become a winner, and they had to know I was going to use every chance I had to rub their noses in it. I was no longer the one they could pity and look down on to make themselves feel better. I'd become a winner and I was feeling quite conceited about it, but my premature smirk was soon wiped, as my best friend seemed incredibly uncomfortable around me. With a forced smile and artificial conversation, it was as if she had just answered the door to a Jehovah's Witness.

"I'm really happy that you finally got your life sorted out," she said with a condescending smile.

"What are you talking about?" My life hadn't been perfect but I don't remember having any great issues that needed to be 'sorted'. She was the one who complained about things. I had been comfortable in my dead-end job with no relationship prospects. My highlights were when I realised that I hadn't spent my week's pay and fun late-night shopping sprees online when I did. Trust me, someone that simple doesn't have the thought processes to have real issues. She never answered my question.

"I really don't have time to talk you now. Bradley will be home soon and he's under a lot of pressure at work now, so I'd really prefer you not to be here."

"This is seriously about me not having that stupid mark on my arm?"

"Why didn't you just get it?" she said, showing the first sign of my old real friend. "Emily's dead and she didn't see that coming, so why would you believe any of her other drivel?"

"Because I'm watching it play out everywhere I turn, and so are you. And now you're worried she might have been right. You're marked and you can't change that, and it's scaring the shit out of you."

"Don't be ridiculous," she snapped, making me realise I had hit a nerve. "Just leave. I have no time for hoodoo rubbish and I don't want to see you again."

I knew there was no point continuing our conversation – I had my answer. Simone was no longer my friend and unless I attached that barcode to my hand, she was never going to be again. What annoyed me the most was that she had disposed of me before I had enough time to show her the photos I had stored in my phone of my beautiful new house. I couldn't show them off to anyone and that really annoyed me.

Just to make sure I hadn't imagined my parents were treating me as badly as my friends, I decided to drop in and visit them too. It seemed it was not the wisest decision. As I pulled into their flower-lined driveway, they were both pottering around their front garden, the place guaranteed to find them on a bright sunny day. We'd obviously had many nice days as I had never seen so much as a weed or dead blade of grass in their perfectly mowed lawn. The house and yard were immaculately kept to impress their daily string of visitors dropping in for a cup of tea or a nice glass of red. They both continued to work part-time, so I never really understood how they found the time to be so anal about the appearance of their home or how I had ended up so differently to them. They must have celebrated the day they got rid of me. Although I had never thought of it before, perhaps that was why they encouraged me to move into their investment unit. How lucky for me I was untidy enough to be given a place with good cheap rent.

As I got out my car my father hurriedly walked towards me. "Get that car off my driveway," he yelled.

"I just came to say hi!"

"You've said it. Now get rid of that car before it drops oil."

"There is nowhere else to park!" I said, desperately wanting him to suggest somewhere but he didn't.

"You've said what you came here for," answered my mother, barely turning her head to even look at me. "Now off you go, and we'd prefer that you didn't return."

That was it – nothing more was said by any of us. I just jumped back into my car praying desperately it had leaked some oil on their precious driveway, but I don't think it did. So off I drove. My question had been answered in no uncertain terms. I no longer had friends or parents, a change in circumstances I was just going to have to learn to live with. The people that I once thought had my back had disowned me just because I didn't have a tattoo stamped onto my hand.

Perhaps people were starting to regret rushing into self-branding and they envied those of us who were unmarked. They couldn't change what they had done so it was easier to just turn against those of us that hadn't. They were scared and now resentful of me. If they now began feeling sorry for themselves, Emily's theory of the marked burning in hell would be coming to roost. The next step may have already begun.

My own new theory was that by treating the unmarked badly, they hoped we might eventually join them and all be destined for damnation. It helped me to feel sorry for those who treated me badly, instead of just hating them with a passion – my earlier choice. It was really hard to hate my parents but at least now I could just think of them as sad cases instead of evil people who had turned against their only child.

Maybe in time all this would settle down and I could happily make up with all the people who had turned on me without having constant evil thoughts about them. They had just been scared. I could forgive that, I thought. I would still abuse them but I wouldn't hold it against them forever. Visiting Simone and my parents had turned out to be quite therapeutic. I had somehow turned bad news into good, and I'd found a new way to deal with my fears – pity everyone around me.

Arriving home to share my epiphany with Michael, I nearly rear-ended a shiny new automobile in the driveway. We never had visitors, so could this amazing luxury car be another gift from my beloved? I was learning to dream big when it came to Michael, and again he didn't disappoint. With a smirk on his face, he threw a set of keys towards me. I've never been a great catch but I would have thought at least I had enough of a sense of self-preservation to protect my face – I didn't! Blood began streaming down my nose, the expensive leather keyring planted firmly in the only piece of dirt on the property in front of me.

"Sorry," pleaded Michael, as he raced over to help me. "Really sorry, but I really don't have the time to keep fixing your piece of crap car. And let's be honest, your work colleagues aren't racing out to help you anymore." There was no need to reply. I just chose to give him a loving hug and, as payback, smear blood all over his favourite white shirt. Unfortunately he now knew me too well.

"I don't care," he sniggered. "You do all the washing."

"Yes, but not very well," I replied excitedly, knowing I'd actually beaten him for a change.

Luckily I'd always kept a rag in my car to wipe the windscreen as the unstable demister wasn't always up to the job. After wiping the blood from my face, I climbed into my flashy new SUV with its all-leather interior and way more technology than I felt I would ever have to use. Looking back at my poor little compact through the ginormous screen that filled half my dashboard, I began to understand the power trip of the many SUV drivers that had once caused me so much annoyance. I felt a bit like God too. It was very adorable having Michael in the passenger seat trying to explain the new high-tech dashboard to me. I probably should have been listening to him, but I was too busy trying to find the radio button and CD player.

"They don't have them anymore," said Michael, as if I was so behind the times to not know, especially when I worked in the automotive industry.

"But you have them," I said, bitterly disappointed.

"My car is old, not as old as yours, obviously."

"What do you mean old as mine – seen what I drive now?"

I still could not understand why new cars would be without a CD player or radio. They didn't take up much room and not everybody owned a smart phone, especially the older people who could afford these new cars. My parents loved their CDs and so did I. I'd stolen my father's really cool movie themes CD – well, I'd only borrowed it – but I was not going to return it now they weren't talking to me. A bit of 'Close Encounters' on the drive home I often found strangely relaxing.

Simone used to tell me that I should put all my CDs onto my phone through the computer and Bluetooth it in the car. It was much simpler just pressing 'go' on the CD, and I would assume it would be the same with a radio. Now I was going to need my phone to hear music or news in my new car. Did the car manufacturers have huge shares in Apple or something? My driving was now going to be in silence, but it didn't matter. I was no longer going to have to drown out the rattling of my old heap of junk.

With no radio in my car, the only place I had ever listened to it, I hadn't noticed the new campaign against those of us without the luminous tattoo. Michael on the other hand had the pleasure of hearing it daily and it was beginning to bother him a great deal. He would explain it to me in a tone that left me with an uneasy feeling. After an advertisement ending with the new common slogan of 'only available with the code' the new way to divide us. The radio announcers would continue with snide remarks implying that the tattooed would be the only ones that mattered. Occasionally, discussions turned to how ridiculously uncoded people were behaving by not conforming and how we were holding back progress by costing the world billions to accommodate us. Or they would explain that we were the reason for so many job losses and were holding back growth. It seemed as though even Michael was starting to believe them.

"Really, why don't we just get the stupid mark?" he said cautiously. "Who cares if Emily was right? At least we could have the life we deserve. What if what they're saying is true and it's us causing all the problems somehow?"

"Seriously? Us not being marked has caused supermarkets, banks and every other industry that can get away with it to cut staff? Doubt that! And I'm fairly sure uncoded criminals aren't the only ones behind the huge increase in thefts. Every computer nerd or hacker

I've ever known was among the first to get that barcode implanted, Justin included."

"I know. Common sense says you're right but it's getting really hard to hold out, especially when I don't really know why I am," he almost pleaded. "I'm not religious and if God wants to make his followers suffer this crap, I'd rather end up in hell anyway."

As most of the unmarked were Christians, discrimination against them was building. It was beginning to look like we were all going to be fed to lions in a coliseum. Luckily there were no scary beasts left for their entertainment. I don't know why I couldn't just go and get that stupid barcode put into my hand either. I still didn't really believe it was Satan's mark so I wasn't holding out for redemption, and I'd always prided myself on being a sheep following the crowd, taking the easy way out. I don't know why I couldn't do it this time, but the more the world turned against me, the more I wanted to fight them.

I think I understood how smokers like Emily felt; every time she saw another news story telling her where she couldn't smoke, she lit one up. I really had begun following Emily's lead. It just felt like I was giving that middle finger salute to those that had overstepped their boundaries. I'd become a rebel like her and the more detrimental to my safety it was becoming, the less chance I had of stopping myself. I was enjoying myself immensely. I think my late friend may have possessed me. It was her personality I was exhibiting, not my boring, go-with-the-flow one at all. Luckily Michael still loved whatever person I had become, and his resistance to the mark continued just for me. What an amazing man I had found. Why couldn't life have just been normal?

000-07-000

THINGS BEGAN TO DECLINE at an unrealistic pace. Problems that should have taken decades to arrive were now unfolding into catastrophes overnight. The droughts that had always occurred were now somehow causing irreparable damage in weeks rather than years. There did not seem to be more natural disasters than usual, but we had lost the ability to overcome them. I wondered if it was stupidity or intentional. Naturally, the third world suffered the most as food shortages were becoming a global problem.

Without help from the rest of the world, countries throughout Africa, Asia and South America were now turning to bushmeat. Poachers for Chinese medicine were no longer a threat as there were barely any animals left to poach. Countries that produced cattle and other livestock charged obscene prices to export their meat throughout the world and inflated the costs of their own local supermarkets too. Even well-established western countries found meat so expensive that they turned to hunting their wildlife as well. Australia exhausted its population of kangaroos. Deer populations throughout the world plummeted at an astonishing rate. The rate of death by snakebite and other animal-related fatalities grew as inexperienced people tried to catch them for food.

Unfortunately for the animals that fought back, there were too many hungry humans and their populations were decimated. I don't think anyone kept score, but I'd say for every person an animal knocked off, thousands of their species were eradicated in return. Animals were seriously disadvantaged against the weapon-carrying humans – it was never going to be a fair fight.

Once again, all this new mess was blamed on us supposed religious freaks without the code. No explanation needed – just tell people something enough times and they will believe you.

Farmers who now seemed destined to be the rulers of this new world needed to produce more animals for consumption, and fast, so scientists came up with exciting new ways to boost production. Unfortunately, they hadn't had the time to iron out any problems and managed to almost wipe out their remaining stocks with a virus they accidentally introduced. Their idea had been to use IVF in a way that would cause cattle, sheep, pigs, even chickens, to have multiple births and shorter gestation times.

The animals' welfare was never considered. They just needed more food, and quickly. The technology that sounded like such a great idea was quickly shared throughout the world. Their mistake wasn't realised for a few months, but when the new animals started arriving, they brought with them an illness that quickly wiped out their farms. Paddocks, once filled with livestock, were now desolate or quickly repurposed to grow vegetables, a much wiser move considering the fact that they had no idea how to control the new monster that they had created, or any idea of how far it would go.

It had all but wiped out the world's farmed animals and the new great idea was to catch and farm the few remaining wild ones. Wild deer, buffalo, feral pig and whatever else had not already been hunted to extinction by the public were captured to farm. But they too succumbed to this evil virus. It was as if the land had stored it like anthrax, just waiting for the next species to infect. The planet as we knew it was becoming a complete animal-free zone, but it was only the loss of food they supplied that seemed to bother anyone. Animal activists who should have been all over the news had become non – existent. Like the religious freaks that once littered the streets, they too had disappeared.

It seemed that two of the scientists working on the original project were unmarked, and supposedly they had secretly infected this new technology with some concocted virus or bacteria to bring on Armageddon. The men swore that it wasn't true and promised that they could prove it, but with no help from their colleagues, they were never given the chance and were paraded around like monsters on every television station.

Showing a new wave of adult bullying at its extreme, millions of faceless people directed messages of hate and disdain through every Twitter, Instagram or Facebook post at a couple of people they knew absolutely nothing about. These men were tried and convicted long before they could ever plead their case in a court of law. They were portrayed as demons and there was no-one left to question the world's behaviour towards them.

These were two middle-aged unassuming nerds, pleading their innocence. Their wives and children could be seen screaming uncontrollably, watching the strangely archaic treatment of their loved ones. The handling of these men was like a return to the dark ages where people were executed and displayed to the cheering public. They had not been proven guilty of anything, but the global lynch mob didn't care. You felt that at any time these two men were going to be buried up to their neck and stoned to death by the large crowds abusing them. From the glass bottles being thrown at them now, I was sure the crowds would have enjoyed the opportunity. The news reports were akin to those being sent from war zones.

I had a strong feeling that I had seen one of these men before in the paper – well, on the internet – there were no more newspapers in circulation. They had all gone exclusively online and were only available through subscription. Our subscription was only still valid because we had paid in advance. Like the majority of the population we were not intending to renew. There was no point – news and opinions were available for free on the web. The newspapers had actually contributed to their own demise, a once powerful medium now irrelevant. My missing radio gave me the feeling that another one was following closely behind.

I remembered who one of the evil scientists that presumably initiated Armageddon was. He had memorably crooked teeth and an unforgettable name – Bartholomew Scrod. Before the mark he had been considered a hero, finding a cure to the incurable multiple sclerosis and getting close to a cure for Parkinson's disease – hardly a man wanting to end the world. It was as if the world had completely forgotten his achievements.

When I looked up his name on the net, I could find nothing of his achievements, only the supposed evil he had just unleashed on the world. It was as if neither of them had existed before that day. Looking back through the online papers, his name and photos had mysteriously disappeared from the story of his great scientific discovery. As everything now was online, there was no paper proof of anything. Someone's entire past removed forever by some high-tech authority or criminal – the lines were becoming very blurred.

The two men never made it to trial. It seemed there was never any intention that they would and the strange parading them around was just a set-up to make it easy for some nutcase to shoot them both dead on live television to the applause of cheering crowds who lifted the shooter up as their hero. He was never charged, but his supposed heroics were plastered on every internet site and television and reported on the rapidly diminishing radio broadcasts. How did this happen? Why was I the only one that noticed some nut had killed a legend? I'd say those cured of MS remembered what he'd done for them and those still suffering Parkinson's knew precisely what they had lost, but there was no mention anywhere. The digital age, where opinions could never be muffled and secrets were always exposed, wasn't living up to its expectations.

With no Facebook friends left or Twitter followers to reach out to, everything I wrote was deleted in minutes. I don't know how they did it but if I shared anything more exciting than what I'd eaten for breakfast, I noticed it soon gone. I assume this was the case for anyone with a sceptical opinion because there was never anything critical about taking the mark – only bad things about the unmarked could ever be found.

In a world where information was now completely located in cyberspace, things could just disappear without a trace. At the same time stupid things many innocents may have wished to be gone could not be erased, no matter how hard one tried. Like the embarrassing teenage photographs that I so never wanted Michael to see, but enter my name and there they were, every time. When I was a teenager I was warned not to upload things but you never really believe that they are going to haunt you for life. Of course no innocent photos of me could be found, just the drunken, wet t-shirt type were all that remained.

The nail was now fully in the coffin of those of us who had resisted the need to be branded. We were now forced to buy absolutely everything online as cards had become obsolete overnight. There was no longer a need to accommodate us. It was now glaringly obvious that we were scheming together to bring the world to its eventual demise. The public had their proof after two innocent scientists were publicly condemned for having diminished the world's greatest source of food. If they really wanted to bring on the end, why didn't they just pollute the world's drinking water? They were presumably clever enough, and it would have sped up the process.

Luckily Michael and I were well used to purchasing everything online as it had become extremely embarrassing paying for our groceries in a supermarket, with snide remarks when we pulled a card from our wallet. Rudeness was no longer the domain of the underclass. It was now an acceptable response for anyone coming across one of the unmarked. Parents would applaud their children calling us offensive names, and the elderly were more than comfortable suggesting we fuck off. Good people seemed to be turning bad at an accelerated rate.

To be honest, apart from Michael, I did not know any other unmarked people. I had occasionally seen them around, looking as uneasy walking the streets as I was, but I never actually bothered to speak to them, and they did not approach me either. Maybe we should have found a way to join forces and uncover the deceit that surrounded us but, to be honest, I never saw anywhere near enough of us to even bother.

My life now revolved around an extremely uncomfortable day at work, followed by the safe, warm feeling I had at home with Michael. With no friends or visitors, safety was becoming a little boring, so we decided to fill our weekends with travel around the countryside in the new car. With fuel in our tank from Michael's business and a cooler box filled with drinks and food, we managed to amuse ourselves for a good couple of weeks.

Unfortunately, one full tank of fuel will only get you so far, and so far becomes very monotonous very quickly, especially when you know a little more could get you to much more exciting destinations, like the lake Michael remembered fishing in as a child and the nature walks I'd remembered from my past. We would desperately try to come up with ways of getting to these destinations to no avail. There were still only so many jerry cans we could safely carry in what was a surprisingly small boot for such a large car. Perhaps the 'wonderful places' would have been disappointing anyway – just exaggerated childhood memories for both of us. Still it would have been nice in our current situation.

I would spend hours online looking up amazing holiday destinations we were actually in a position to afford, but unfortunately purchasing the tickets would have been as far as we could have gone. Every detail of people's ticket purchases was scanned from their computer into their hand, to be rescanned at the airport, concerts, zoo, any event. Passports too were irrelevant. They were now imprinted into your hand forever. The do-it-yourself thing had become quite common at airports with only a few Customs staff left, purely for the job of scanning your luggage. We had been processing our own passports for a while anyway. More of that diminishing employment bubble Emily had been pointing out.

So holidays too were now just a dream, and I was sure it wasn't going to be long before they began making everyone scan their hand for every computer purchase. Then we would be total goners. If Michael and I were having so many problems, I could only imagine the pain and suffering of others unable to even purchase fuel. What hell they must have been going through. It's not as if they were able to catch public transport as it too now relied on one scanning their hand. So how did they get around? I don't think they did, hence the fact I barely ever saw them.

The government still gave some assistance to those unemployed with the mark, while leaving those without to completely fend for themselves. With no employment and therefore no money, even if they had a home, they would have been unable to afford running power or amenities. They would have been left with no other choice but to steal food from households, as supermarkets would have had a lot more security.

My disturbing prediction soon became reality. Homes were now constantly broken into by this new underclass taking anything they could get their hands on. I say 'they' and yet I could easily have become one of them had my situation been a little different and had I not met Michael, my shining light.

There was not a home that hadn't been scarred by this new crime wave that had taken over our world. Despite CCTV and no mark, we were not immune from the new scourge. On many occasions we arrived home to find our fridge and cupboards bare, a deeply annoying problem for people who couldn't just race down to the shops to refill our stocks. We'd have to go hungry until our next online delivery arrived, generally the next day.

It wasn't just the fact that our food and things were missing, although that was extremely annoying, but strangers had invaded our home. Our safe had been robbed almost every time we walked out the door. It left you feeling violated and angry at the perpetrators. We soon realised that everything had to be delivered to Michael's factory. Left outside it would be gone before we arrived home.

Our decent clothes had to travel to work with us as it was becoming very expensive to replace them every couple of weeks. Our television and furniture were very large, making them hard to steal, so my beautiful mansion looked like a ghost house, bereft of any pictures, décor or personal mementos. Anything we loved was hidden at Michael's factory which was incredibly secure and possibly ignored as there would be no assumption of it housing food of any kind.

No wonder we had become so hated. I too now despised the unmarked. They were just low-life criminals, taking everything we loved and needed to survive. Finally I had someone to look down upon, as I hadn't sunk to their level. I too was missing the mark, but I hadn't turned to crime. It was a terrible feeling knowing when you left for work each day there was a big chance unwanted visitors were pillaging your home. The place one should be able to feel safe and secure had now become a one-stop shop for thieves. Investing in guard dogs was no longer an option and the thought of staying at home to fight them off seemed fraught with danger. These were desperate and hungry people so we assumed they would be prepared for confrontation and probably well-armed to deal with it. All we could really do was hope that leaving nothing for them to steal would eventually cause them to reconsider coming.

We were extremely lucky to have the option of a factory for storage. I could only imagine how frustrating and annoying it would be for the many who didn't. Knowing that your property and supposed safe haven was going to be robbed on a daily basis was incredibly stressful and created intense feelings of anger towards the perpetrators. We had their images on film, but they were always completely covered from balaclavas to hijabs and always wearing gloves. We all assumed it was to hide the fact that they were unmarked but even I was slow to realise the obvious fact – the reason for the gloves was to hide their marks.

The police never bothered to look for them or the stolen goods. It had become an epidemic that no-one could stop. They knew that there was no point even trying.

I was truly beginning to side with the masses and believe the many stories of the atrocities perpetrated by the unmarked, from stealing the few remaining pets to robbing graves of the recently departed, in their search for the now very limited supply of meat. These people were beyond evil, I thought. How had someone at work not knocked me off yet? Maybe I needed the mark so I wouldn't turn into one of these degenerates. Still internally debating my strange aversion to not receiving the mark, I overheard a conversation at the office between some of the senior staff. Thinking nobody could hear them they spoke freely about their weekend visit to a one-time puppy farm that was now making a fortune selling the meat from their now-useless breeding animals and puppies bred before the virus had taken hold.

One mentioned that the wealthy were able to visit old horse studs and pick themselves up a truly decent cut of meat. They were casually discussing why they had already eaten their beloved pets –

cats and dogs were never really going to handle vegetarianism – so it was out of sympathy they slaughtered and ate them. They explained to their children their beloved pets must have been stolen by the evil unmarked that had been regularly robbing their homes. They never mentioned how they explained away the meat they were feeding to them. Maybe they never shared it.

I hadn't tasted meat in months but I was coping on a steady diet of vegetarian meals. Granted they weren't delicious but I seriously doubt that I could have eaten one of my pets if I had owned one. I'm not sure the virus affected fish stocks, but with meat no longer available, the seas seemed to have emptied. Probably trawled beyond repair or the sea critters had worked out a way to avoid being caught because seafood too was no longer an option.

Now if these people were using the unmarked as their excuse to explain their missing pets to their children, why wouldn't everybody now go along with it? Was it really just the unmarked robbing us blindly? There was no-one left to fight for them or investigate any concocted story that was told about them. The powers that be all seemed to have the mark, so only their side of the story would ever be told.

The great worldwide web was only full of one-sided arguments as I had already proven when I tried to tell Emily's story and look up the evil scientists that had supposedly been the cause of this meat shortage. There was no mention of grave digging in their discussion, possibly for a very good reason as I couldn't imagine anyone wanting to admit that. I drove past a large cemetery daily and I never noticed any signs of disturbance. It was possibly just another rumour created to direct more anger towards the unmarked. They could say what they liked – no-one would ever question it.

Supposedly a whole new underground society had evolved trading in stolen goods and services because, unlike the days of just the poor doing it tough on the streets, this new lot was a mix of talented professionals: tradesman, the occasional doctors, lawyers and pretty well any profession you could think of. I found it amazing that people who had once had so much hadn't worked out how to bypass this strange new world as well as Michael and I had. I still had a job and Michael was still in charge of a reasonably large business. Life wasn't easy but we managed by buying everything online. I couldn't understand how someone who'd once earned so much money could have none left or how people so important could lose their jobs, but they did.

Being unmarked myself put me in the perfect position to investigate so I did or at least attempted to. Because walking the city streets without that illuminating tag on one's hand was now an invitation to ridicule and potential danger, I decided it might be the perfect way to get noticed by others in my predicament. I'd watched far too many movies where people just happened to be saved by someone on their side hiding down a dark alley as if they had just been waiting there, intent on rescuing some poor lost soul. Well I tried it, and it seems the fairytale is absolute crap. Granted I only made it to the street corner, but I'm fairly sure that there was no-one waiting around to save me. Those with luminous marked hands that passed me by did not harass me. I was just looked down upon in a way that made me feel very unsafe and insecure. Not one other unmarked hand for as far as the eye could see, and although I was not spat on or abused, I just knew that I wasn't welcome there. So, after my very brief visit back in the real world, I cautiously sauntered back to the safety of my company's underground car park, jumped into my car and burst into a tidal wave of tears.

What the hell was going on? Not that long ago I had walked that street with my head held high, like some invincible superhero – my blonde locks swinging with confidence and a twinkle in my eyes every time a suited man, or anyone for that matter, gave me a smile. Granted my hair was no longer as blonde as it had been. I was too scared to approach my old hairdresser friends, and that confidence I once exuded never had any real substance behind it. With Michael in my corner, I was now actually in a position to flaunt that conceited persona that I had created back then, but instead I scurried away like a mouse dumped into the middle of a snake pit.

If I had just gotten that tattoo, I could be like them again, all those people walking the streets with my old confidence, but that's not how they looked. People walking through the city in the past generally just gave the impression that they were in a hurry to be somewhere because they were so wrapped up in their own importance, but not this time. Now they walked with more desperation, in a hurry to save their job or in fear of the small unmarked woman walking towards them. As they approached, their fear turned to anger and hatred. I could almost feel their temperature rising. Is that what I would have become? A person full of more hatred than I could ever understand?

I had reneged on that tattoo for completely different reasons than the majority of the unmarked. I had no deep religious convictions and, to be honest, no real idea at all. Maybe I abstained so I could see through clear eyes what was really going on out there. In the beginning I think I did it for Emily, and maybe I eventually noticed so much injustice that I had to see this through and stick to my guns. Yeah, I'd finally become someone with principles.

It would have been cleverer to have just joined Greenpeace or some save-the-world group but I generally found them irritating. As I'd just worked out that I may have had a smidgen of superhero in me, I decided that I was ready to face my once incredibly sensible old buddies, and to the hair salon I drove. It was only a ten minute walk from my car park but there wasn't enough hero in me to face the scary street again.

Luckily I found a car space directly in front of the salon as I really wouldn't have had the courage to walk any further. As I slithered my way into the shop, flinching from the burning stares of their customers, I attracted Jackie's attention.

"Go out to the back room," she hurriedly waved me off. "Dean or I will see you when we have a minute."

"Ok." I disappeared behind the half door separation, as I watched Jackie and Dean quietly trying to explain my appearance to their unimpressed customers. This was once a place I used to prance around like a prima donna, pirouetting onto any available seat and making small talk with every client. I once brought life and a bit of amusement into the place, now I was banished to the naughty corner, awaiting my uncertain punishment. I didn't remember this type of fear during my school years, and I certainly wasn't the perfect student.

"I'm not a six year old." I mumbled, bored with watching the loudly ticking clock that was ten minutes behind. Jackie quickly appeared as if to silence me. "Your clock's out."

"I know," she replied quietly. "Don't you remember setting it that way to trick the customers into thinking we weren't running late."

"Oh yeah, did it ever work?"

"No, but I don't have the heart to change it. I'd like something to remember you by."

"I'm not dead!"

"I'm sorry but unless you get that mark, you have to be to us. We run a business and can't afford to be associated with someone unmarked. I'm so sorry but at least we know you're safe and well looked after with Michael. If you ever decide to receive the mark, best friends again I promise, but until that happens we just can't associate with you."

"Would you treat Emily the same way?" I asked, knowing they had liked her more.

"Seriously, Elisha, this isn't because we don't like you, and if Emily was still here, behaving in the same manner as you, which I'm positive she would be, we wouldn't be able to associate with her either. Grab yourself a cold drink from the fridge, and there's a plate of those homemade cookies that you love over there. We're closing up soon so we can have a bit of a chat."

I wasn't sure what she meant by that as she'd already made her case and our friendship was obviously over. No big surprise there, so why keep the enemy around. Maybe she and Dean were some type of terminators secretly using cookies to knock off the unmarked who were unfortunate enough to venture into their shop. Strange thoughts to have about old friends that I would happily have sent my children to live with, but things everywhere now were out of the norm.

If my fate were to be death by cookie, it would have been quick, as I'd demolished the entire plate within fifteen minutes. They were the best biscuits, and knowing I would never see them again made them taste so much better than I remembered. Jackie had actually given me the recipe once, and I followed it precisely but they just didn't taste the same. I often found that with food, somebody else's always tastes better than your own even on the many occasions I used to visit the shop and the staff would offer me their take-away hot chips from down the road. They were so good I'd go to the exact store to buy my own, and they were always inferior to the ones I had just eaten. Maybe there was some underlying criminal in my make-up as I always found that others' food was always better than mine. The thief inside was just waiting to rear its ugly head, and maybe a life of crime was my true destiny. I didn't really want to be forced into finding out.

"Why did you come here?" Dean asked me with a confused look on his face. It was as though I were a murderer taking refuge in their tiny back room, not a once-great friend who had dropped in for a visit to catch up.

"So I could ask you a question," I replied, filled with spite and a bit of criminal intent, "but there's no need now. I'm fairly sure I know the answer. Sorry to have ruined your day. Oh, and I ate all your cookies," I added, rising to leave and satisfied that I had polished off the cookies I knew he loved as much as I did. He gently grabbed me by the arm and with a slight look of regret asked me to stay until Jackie was finished. "But there's no more cookies left," I told him abruptly. Then he pulled another of the many plates of cookies from out of the cupboard, handing them to me.

"It's not safe to leave them at home anymore," he said with a glare, "as your lot just keep stealing our short supply of food." Jackie appeared before I had a chance to defend myself, which was handy as I hadn't really come up with a good comeback.

"Elisha, you have to understand the trouble we have had with unmarked people like you. Our house is constantly being robbed, and it's becoming really hard to afford replacing our food so often, especially with the extra security we've installed, and this place is barely supporting us."

"Just so you know," I replied, "our house is constantly broken into too, and are you really that sure that every time it's someone unmarked? I mean let's be honest. There is still an awful lot of unemployed out there now, and I don't think having the mark turns you all into trustworthy, virtuous people. I'm fairly sure that serial killers, drug dealers and paedophiles haven't changed their ways just because they were stamped on the hand. Not every criminal out there is missing the mark. You know those news stories that don't mention an unmarked perpetrator, it's because they have the mark even though they always display them with a jacket over their arms. Any idiot should be able to work out why."

"That I have noticed," said Jackie, turning to Dean. "Remember I mentioned it?" He just shrugged his shoulders with disinterest. "But there is no reason for marked people to be stealing our food because the ever-increasing taxes on our incomes are being used to support them." I had to nod in agreement to that one. I had also noticed my income shrinking steadily.

"But none of it is going to the unmarked," I added. "So maybe everything wrong with this world isn't just our fault."

"The major things are," said Dean, "and that's enough for us to not want you around."

"Many unmarked are doctors, lawyers, nurses, builders," I began. "You think they all just became dangerous because they didn't want a barcode embedded into their hand. And how are so many of them now living without money? That I really don't understand. People at work say that they have a criminal underground going where they trade our stolen goods."

"Our local GP didn't receive the mark," said Jackie, a little down, "He had recently invested in expensive property that he was soon forced to sell at a big loss, leaving him nothing but debt and a practice that we all stopped using because he didn't have the mark."

"So you screwed over your own doctor," I suggested to a couple who almost looked guilty for a minute.

"You and Michael have just been extremely lucky," Jackie said. "You won't be for much longer – soon you won't be able to order things online without the mark. They are soon going to force everyone to scan their hand to make a purchase. No mark, no purchase, so you'll be getting that barcode soon or get used to a life of crime. I don't think you're that sneaky or holding out on the mark for a good enough reason to put up with too much suffering."

"You have the mark and you're obviously no happier than me."

"Whatever," replied Jackie. "You're no longer one of us, and unless you get that hand of yours barcoded, you never will be again, and we can't have anything to do with you. Right, wrong or indifferent, it's the way things are, so please never come here again because next time we won't be so courteous."

With that I left, no goodbye, certainly no "see you later", but I did grab the plate of cookies so my visit had not been a complete failure.

So that was it. I no longer had family or friends, a position that would have mortified me before I knew Michael. Having him made all the others seem insignificant. They were yesterday's garbage and I found it amazing that I could throw them away with such ease. Was it because they were the ones that threw me away first with no obvious signs of regret? Or was it because I now had someone that bought me safety and happiness in a way they never could? This being-in-love thing was amazing, and with most of the world against us, incredibly exciting in a strange way. Was I avoiding the mark to keep this special bond between us so intense and a little bit dangerous, keeping us at arms-length from the others and inadvertently forcing us closer?

I often thought I was batting above my average with Michael, and I knew him being unmarked was a guaranteed way of stopping his chances of finding someone else. Could this be why I was set on torturing both of us? I'd found my perfect man and mastered the art of keeping him hostage without him realising what was going on. No, I wasn't that clever or imaginative. I couldn't get marked because I'd now seen too much – things I'm sure I would have missed had I just followed the masses. What I could do with this knowledge was negligible but I could see the truth, and again for no good reason, had to see where it was leading.

The world, or at least the small part that I had access to, had become a strange place. There were no longer problems associated with bird faeces on the windscreen as there were no longer any birds – well, none that I ever came across anymore. I hadn't even noticed their decline, but one day Michael mentioned that he had noticed one of his employees eating something that looked like unappetising chicken. He was informed it was a pigeon.

With access to new, idiot-proof weapons, people were hunting down the wildlife – flocks of birds decimated in minutes by amateur hunters. Although I hadn't noticed the absence of the birds initially, now I really missed them. They had never been something that particularly interested me, but I had enjoyed the times I came across them. The beautiful or more often annoying sounds that echoed through the air when birds were around had all gone. I remembered those sounds with great fondness and longed to hear them again.

Of course with the lack of predators, bugs and spiders now seemed to reign supreme, and vermin were quickly taking over the streets – their population only slightly controlled by the fact that they were about our only remaining source of meat.

I'm not sure if it was intentional but humans, like rats and mice, seemed to have an immunity to this new disease. Could we be considered the new vermin? I never heard anyone else bring up that theory but a lot must have considered it. Luckily for me I'd adopted to the vegetarian lifestyle fairly easily and the need to eat rats never entered my mind. We had just taken the planet to a scary place and I think we all knew that it couldn't end well. Or was it just me with only Michael to talk to?

Nothing was ever reported of the damage we were doing, which I found strange, since years before people were constantly protesting against environmental damage. Once you could switch on the news to see a thousand people trying to save a couple of trees, but where were all these people hiding now that we were wiping out one species after another? Where had all the political activists disappeared to, and why were they not fighting for us? The world had been bursting at the seams with human rights activists begging us to take in refugees, apologising for our centuries old behaviour to the less fortunate. Trying to persuade us to accept people with different skin colours, religions, sexual orientations and anything else that I'm fairly sure we had already accepted, but never well enough for them.

This time they really had a good cause to follow with the unmarked being so completely and obviously persecuted, but nothing was ever mentioned. Not a word from them. Were we that irrelevant, or just that evil that we weren't worth trying to save? Or maybe they just knew that there was nothing they could do to help this time. Still strange when nothing else they ever did made any difference anyway. I think the real reason for their silence was that the unmarked were never going to gain any sympathy from the marked, no matter how much anyone tried, or maybe they too were all marked and their slogans of justice and fairness for all somehow didn't include us.

That didn't explain their silence on the diminishing jungles and animal populations of the world – nothing but silence. Activists hadn't actually been wiped off the planet like I'd first thought as they still showed up occasionally on the news reports, parading around with banners to protest irrelevant crap like trying to stop new buildings going ahead and seeking better pay deals for some obscure government department. They thought that was worth complaining about, but the demise of the world as we once knew it, wasn't? It was a scary time that made no real sense at all.

New technology had given us access to the world: an information highway where we could google an answer to almost anything we wanted to know. It had been a place where opinions could be heard and shared. People's views were still accessible but none of them seemed to differ too much, and they were always about irrelevant junk, never anything about what was really going on in the world.

It seemed as if this new social network had become a pointless discussion tool for a group of simple-minded zombies. The daily news reports were no better, giving us limited information on anything worth hearing. They would at least mention the fact that unemployment was getting out of hand and that our new vegetarian lifestyle was here to stay, but it was always blamed on the unmarked and there was never anyone anywhere to defend us.

Real information had now become extremely hard to access and, with no libraries or books to reference, a lot of the past seemed to have disappeared into the internet abyss. Like many things we had become so dependent on, when new technology turned on many of us, we had left ourselves nowhere else to go.

It was no longer just the unmarked needing to trade goods and services underground. With so much unemployment, the black market was taking hold everywhere and subsequently hurting the taxman as less and less people were making this new cyberspace money and therefore government revenue was dropping. Unemployed people were still receiving a small amount of help and free electricity so they could at least access their funds as it became obvious that without electricity, there were no transactions at all. No power, no scanners, no money. What an interesting world we had created for ourselves? A new world that seemed to be rapidly going backwards. Not that we could find history books to remind us. If we were returning to the days of the caveman, which was looking inevitable, we were going to do it a lot differently since there was nothing left to hunt.

I really missed Emily but I sometimes wondered whether even she would have lacked the courage to avoid the dreaded mark. In some ways it made me happy that she didn't have to suffer this. I remembered back to one of our conversations when I'd been having a bad day. I suggested I was so unlucky that if I'd ever won the lottery, I'd pick up my winnings and get hit by a truck. Turns out I had some clairvoyance in me. Meeting Michael was my lucky lotto moment, and the world turned upside down straight after. I probably would have preferred the truck. At least it would have been swift.

To be honest, the way life was now panning out I'd probably survive the crash and lose all feeling from the neck down or be trapped in a vegetative state with a fully alert mind but a body that could do nothing. Able to hear and see all that is going on, while being constantly tortured by being unable to say or do anything. I became glad that I'd had this horrific thought because it gave me that extra will to keep fighting, realising that no matter how scary my situation was becoming, there was always a lot worse.

One way to pull yourself out of a depressed state is to imagine the many more ghastly situations you could be in. I should have become a shrink. I could have cured a lot of sad people, but then again, I assume the psychiatric fraternity had already given my method a try at some stage and proved its failure. It was irrelevant as it worked for me, which was handy, because it's not like I had the option of visiting a psychiatrist anyway.

000-08-000

FOR EVERY BAD DAY, occasionally a good one would appear. I was eating my lunch at my desk. Unwelcome in the lunchroom and unable to purchase food elsewhere, I now had the pleasure of taking a little cooler bag, filled with a cut sandwich and a few cans of soft drink. It was a cheaper option but boring, especially when the person returning to the office with the lunch run started handing out food that looked and smelt a lot more exciting than mine.

I'm not sure how they worked out who paid for what. They must have all ordered separately online and paid up front on the computer because I doubt the lunch runner would have liked to pay for everyone's meals and rely on them paying him back. It wasn't as if people had become more financially responsible for paying their own way. Even when it was my job, I often had to suffer the IOUs because people were without cash in their wallets. But I soon learnt that they never intended to pay me back, so if they didn't have the money up front, I just wouldn't get their lunch.

Even as a general non-cash user myself, it annoyed me when the others didn't have it. You never actually missed something until it was no longer an option. This particular day a young male employee had returned to work with a bag of lunch goodies, and instead of the usual complete ignorance of my existence, he was actually heading towards me. I thought he had taken pity and bought me a treat or something as he strolled towards me with a grin, flicking the hair from his eyes as his hands were full of goodies. I had a slight giggle at one stage when he nearly lost his balance. He didn't appreciate the smile on my face, which made me realise that he wasn't on his way over to be nice.

"I met your friend Simone down the shop," he said. I didn't bother telling him that I no longer had any friends. I was surprised that he hadn't already worked that out. "Bradley lost his job."

Unfortunately for him that was never going to be news that would wipe that earlier smile off my face. I said nothing as he stormed off, obviously deflated, which helped to increase my grin, showing the teeth that had only been displayed at home for as long as I could remember. No – there was also the time when I stole Jackie and Dean's cookies!

It seemed that the despair of my ex-friends was now the only source of happiness for me apart from Michael. How twisted I'd become. Had Bradley lost his job when we were still friends, I wouldn't have been any less excited, but back then he could have found another one. Nowadays, maybe not.

Unlike Michael and myself, Bradley and Simone would still be looked after to some degree by the government, and Bradley would surely have made some provisions for his future, I thought. The way he threw around money and behaved like there was a never-ending supply, he certainly should have. I would never know for sure, so there was no point wasting my time feeling sorry for them. I hadn't really become uncaring. I knew that they would be fine, but I could still enjoy the fleeting thought that maybe they weren't. A little evil but not if I truly believed that they were ok. Well, that was my excuse.

Relaying the happy news to Michael, I was a little surprised he wasn't sharing my enthusiasm as I knew he wasn't really a fan of Bradley's either.

"Have you seen the news today?" Michael interrupted my Bradley story.

"I just arrived home and with no radio in my car, of course I haven't. Why?"

"It seems all of your old friends are getting themselves in trouble today."

"What are you talking about?"

"Dean was in a car accident," Michael began. "He accidently ran a red light and cleaned up a family of five, killing them all – three little kids under ten!" Ok that triggered some emotion.

"Is he alright?"

"Yeah, because he was driving a big four-wheel drive and the family were in a stupid, little compact car like your old one. They say he's been charged and probably looking at a fairly long sentence."

"For running a red light?"

"He killed five people," replied Michael, the anger turning his face a little red. "He has to pay for that."

"He's one of the last people I want to stick up for, but it was obviously an accident. I doubt he woke up in the morning and decided to go out and kill a family. He doesn't drink or take drugs and drive. Actually, I remember him being a ridiculously cautious driver. I don't think I know anyone who hasn't done something stupid on the road. I've run more than one red light in my time."

"But you didn't kill anyone."

"I was lucky. So now you go to prison just because you're unlucky."

"If you kill people, you do."

"Remember last week when you accidently cut off that little mini thing. Had they not quickly got out of your way, you too could be on your way to the lock up."

"Don't be ridiculous."

"I'm just saying I'm sure there was no criminal intent in what Dean did, and I'm almost positive the world isn't going to be a safer place having him locked away. It's just going to ruin another family, and one of the few hard- working taxpayers they have left, just because he accidently ran a red light."

"You're entitled to your opinion," said Michael, showing no interest in what I had to say. "But you're wrong again, so you should probably keep your thoughts to yourself."

It's not like I had anyone else to share them with and being told he no longer wanted to hear them was making me a little worried. Michael was beginning to have trouble at work with his lack of a mark, and there was no denying who was responsible for that. He never said anything or blamed me for the trouble I was obviously causing him but his affection towards me was slowly dwindling away.

The world was truly beginning to resemble a wasteland as the news showed the deterioration of so many countries that Emily had told us amazing things about. We saw footage of unmarked villagers trying to stop large machinery from tearing apart their jungle. It was reported as the unmarked trying to stop essential progress. Most of the footage was covering the occasionally successful spearing by a villager of the well-armed military men destroying their forest. They didn't show the rest of the footage when the soldiers just machine-gunned down the protesters. You didn't see it but you knew it had happened when they never showed another shot of the poor villagers.

The world needed food, and jungles were considered great farming land to feed the masses, which was what they tried to tell us, while demonising the villagers for trying to stop it. Of course, destroying the forests was also the best way to find bushmeat that had been clever enough to avoid man up till then. Such incidents were continually portrayed as the unmarked trying to stop food production, but that wasn't at all what it looked like to me.

Even Michael couldn't decide if he believed them or me, which I found quite concerning as it seemed so obvious, watching half-naked, spear-carrying men trying to fight off the well-armed, military-precision destruction of their land. Was I the only one that noticed the discrepancy, or had I just lost my grip on reality? I didn't have anyone else to ask but the fact was these jungles played an integral part in the system that gives us clean oxygen to breathe. Why was no-one else seeing a problem here. I hadn't lost the plot; the world around me had.

Identity theft had not really disappeared as it continually reared its head in many third-world countries, and over time western civilisation started catching on to it. Again it was blamed on the unmarked, as reports came in of possibly thousands of suspected abductions of people for that mark on their hand.

Many African and Middle Eastern countries already had judicial systems that condoned cutting off limbs. Now they had the opportunity of making it quite profitable. Gangs of marauding criminals were now taking over entire villages, occasionally keeping the people alive until they had cleverly emptied their bank accounts and moved all the funds to their own, or just chopping off their arms and doing it more quickly. The end was the same on all counts. When the money was gone, so too were the people, massacred the minute they were of no further purpose.

Hearing such reports had obviously encouraged many in the western world to follow suit as it soon became a large problem throughout the world. The elderly suffered the most, generally the ones that lived alone, but anyone was fair game. Without the need to have a gang of criminals, a lone person could just turn up on someone's doorstep, force their hand under the scanner on their computer and rob them blind. Generally the first anyone knew about the incident was when someone arrived home to find a loved one deceased. Occasionally their life was spared, but their money was never returned and the perpetrator never arrested.

With no proof or evidence, these incidents were always blamed on the unmarked, as supposedly we were the only ones with the motivation to behave in such an unjust manner. What bothered me was the fact that these people again had to be computer competent to know how to hide the money they had just stolen.

I still remembered how computer geeks rushed to get the mark. To me it was way more obvious that the marked were responsible. It was also a well-reported fact that terrorists, and criminal gangs were quick to take up the mark as well. Before the mark appeared, they would have been the first suspects, so why weren't they now?

They were marked so that made them above the law, or was it just way too convenient to blame everything on unmarked people? I was fairly sure that was exactly what was going on, and even though Michael begrudgingly came around to my theory, he couldn't do anything more about it than I.

My time of avoiding this new marked world was coming to an end with Michael finding it increasingly hard to run his business without it. Although he could basically hide away in his office letting his marked employees deal with customers and ordering, they were now turning against him. His staff were well paid and could always rely on him when they had financial or emotional problems. Seriously, he was a boss anyone would have been blessed to work for and before the arrival of the mark, his employees thought they were. They loved him and would have done anything for him as he would them. I will never understand how Michael's lack of a tattoo turned them around so completely.

They began using blackmail to keep his secret from his once-loyal customers, and there was nothing he could do to stop them. The fact that Michael's business going under would have been the end to their jobs didn't seem to cross their now-disturbed minds. If they sent him broke, they too would be unemployed – another fact that got lost in this strange new world. Michael had pointed it out to them, but they chose not to care and continued to take advantage of his predicament.

The more his staff misbehaved, the greater the likelihood of him receiving that mark. Once marked, Michael could just sack them all, as he knew there would be a long line of talented staff more than happy to take their jobs. Without the mark he could do nothing, even though there were desperate people needing work. They would rather starve than work for someone unmarked. That's how strange life had now become.

We were fortunate that no-one realised unmarked people were living in our house as many others, still fortunate enough to have a property, began suffering immensely. I would drive past properties that were obviously owned by others missing the tattoo as their houses were covered in graffiti pointing out their situation and making them a target for any marked person with a grudge against them. As nearly every marked person had a grudge against us, it was not at all surprising to see people in a Mercedes throwing bags full of excrement at these properties, to cheers and horn blowing from other drivers. The fact that it had to be human didn't seem to bother the crowds. Did it not enter their minds that these obviously well-dressed, wealthy individuals had been collecting their own poo. No-one even cared about yuck anymore, scaring me off that mark even more.

I was beginning to realise that any hopes I had of avoiding this now-obvious-only-to-me evil tattoo were diminishing. Seeing the effects it had on the branded human population made it so much harder to want to join them. I'd watched my family and friends disown me just because I didn't share their mark, completely forgetting the past I had with any of them, even when my parents had far better reasons to do that in my youth.

I remember crashing my father's new car once after taking it without permission. He was incredibly angry with me but I was forgiven because I was his daughter and he supposedly loved me, no matter what. I could ruin his pride and joy with no repercussions, but I was cast out from his life the minute I refused to tattoo myself. There was nothing even slightly natural about that behaviour but it was now the new norm.

I knew secrets about my friends and family that back in the old days could have ruined their relationships or community standing, from Simone and my father's infidelity to Jackie's gambling problems, just to name a few. Yet they were still willing to risk turning against me without even so much as a thought that I might fight back and share their indiscretions with the people they least wanted to know.

They either felt that I was someone they could still trust, making it harder to believe that they would turn on me like that, or I had just become so irrelevant that they knew no-one would ever believe a word I uttered, even knowing I had proof to back my claim. I think the latter was the truth because without that mark I had become completely insignificant to anyone that had it. That was how strange life had turned – with no mark you were now no-one.

If I took that tattoo, would people just talk to me again as if nothing had happened? Would I even remember the horrible way that I had been treated and the way I felt being almost completely disengaged from this new society? That last thought made the whole idea of being marked sound like a fairly agreeable option until that stupid subconscious that I had lost all control of threw more unenviable thoughts back into my mind. Did I really want to forget what I'd seen and been through? My original answer was "yes", but that trouble-making new persona I had unwittingly adopted was forcing me to decide "no". I wasn't going against my better judgment to get that mark, no matter how much easier it would have been.

If I was going to be stuck in this new world with little to no chance of survival without being branded, I was going to have to come up with some amazing new way of getting through this. Then it came to me. I envisaged what I thought to be a wonderful idea. Michael and I still had time and enough money to set ourselves up with a lifetime supply of canned foods while we were still able to shop online.

Mind you, even the online shopping that we'd now been basically forced into for most products had deteriorated from its original form. Things would be delivered months after they had been ordered and paid for, or sometimes just not at all. So the great, quick, easy reliability we had originally been accustomed to was now disappearing when our option of walking into the shop was no longer available. Actually, it had stopped before then but when the alternative disappeared, it just got a lot worse. It often took more time, phone calls and many emails trying to find out why our packages weren't being delivered when they were supposed to be. So much for the quick five minutes to buy something on your phone or computer!

Luckily the superstores sold everything now and their delivery times were a little more reliable. Of course, you could guarantee that once they'd completely wiped all their competition, their service standards wouldn't deteriorate as well. It was something that had already occurred in every other industry.

For now, we could still buy all the camping equipment we needed, so when things became too hard to handle, the two of us could disappear deep into the woods, preferably somewhere near a running stream, and live like hermits together forever.

I actually began looking forward to being completely cut off from this strange new world and knowing nothing more about it. Not having to suffer watching its decline and, most importantly, never having to worry about becoming victim to some scary animal predator as they seemed to be pretty well all gone, making for a boring but much safer existence. We could have made cubby houses above the trees like when we were children, but now with the tools to make a much better job of it. Many people had been living off the grid for years by their own choice so I knew it wasn't an impossible dream until I mentioned it to Michael.

"Seriously?" was his none-too-impressed answer. "That is the most ridiculous idea I have ever heard come out of your mouth. You want to be a hobo? Have fun with that because I certainly won't be joining you."

"So what are we going to do when we can no longer shop online?"

"You got us into this mess, but you're going to have to come up with something better than living in the wilderness to get us out of it," he replied.

"We could be like Tarzan and Jane," I said with a smile.

"What makes you think this is a fucking joke?" His lip quivered in anger before he stormed off, continuing to abuse me as he went. "I gave you everything and you ruined it all. I can't even look at you right now."

I didn't bother arguing because to be honest I didn't really have a comeback. I sort of knew he was right, so nothing I said was going to fix it. We'd had these tiffs before and we usually made up the next day. He left for work before I woke up but I was fairly certain that we would be having great make-up sex that night.

My employment was totally reliant on the amount of business Michael was doing with my company, something I had been aware of because it made perfect sense, and they had already informed me. I was very unpopular and I knew that they were only keeping me because of Michael. Quite sad that from once being a fairly independent person, I had now become completely reliant on my boyfriend. Even my parents had not had that sort of power over my adult life. Although they helped me out occasionally, I could have actually survived without them.

Now my life was wholly dependent on Michael – a situation I would not have chosen to be in, but there it was. My independence was completely gone, a factor I may never have realised had I not been terminated from work. It wasn't the nice 'oh sorry, we have to let you go'. I just got, "Your boyfriend's not doing enough business with us anymore, so pack up your crap and get out of here now."

"Will I get the holiday pay you owe me?" I asked, already knowing the answer.

"Don't be ridiculous," laughed Tim, my boss. "Leave now and don't ever come back here again."

This was the man that I once thought always had my back. With his neatly pressed suit and just enough flecks of grey through his brown hair to give him that trustworthy fatherly appearance, I used to truly believe he'd protect me no matter what. This had been the first time that I had seen him for quite a while. I should have realised he'd been intentionally avoiding me, and to be fair, he kept me around a lot longer than my own father. I felt this unprecedented need to throw up.

"Can I just quickly use the bathroom before I leave?" I asked, through gritted teeth trying to hold back the vomit.

"No, you need to just leave now."

"Fine, fuck you," I replied, heaving up the largest amount of vegetarian green, sticky vomit I had ever seen, with neat yellow corn kernels that I did not remember consuming. It was awesome watching the shock on his face as the green spew dripped onto the white-carpeted floor. The satisfaction was so overwhelming that I almost forgot that I had just lost my job, driving home with a lunar smile across my face.

After happily prancing around my house for a while, the excitement of my little victory began wearing off, and the sad realisation that I had just become unemployed began taking effect. I knew that I would never be able to find another job as there was no chance of being hired without that mark. I was now going to become completely dependent on Michael. I was happy enough to let someone bail me out from time to time but completely relying on them didn't sound like a good idea under any circumstances. This had become a terrible day but mostly because I now needed to vomit again, and again.

After a good hour of spewing, a horrific thought entered my mind and I remembered a pregnancy test that I had bought online a few months ago because it had been on special. It was not an ideal time to be bringing a new life into the world but pregnancy was the only sound reason I could think of to explain my nausea.

The stick turned a positive blue the second it hit my pee. I didn't know if I should be happy or sad. I was just lost, desperately waiting for Michael's return as there was no-one else I could talk to. No family, no friends. I realised how much this was not a good thing. I couldn't bring an innocent baby into this world. I could no longer look after myself. How could I care for someone else? This was tragic news, and I was now in a lot more trouble than I could ever have imagined. My only hope was Michael, the man I had just had a little fight with, but he was still my hero and the only possible person to know how to deal with this situation because it was his problem too. I desperately wanted to call him but I knew that this wasn't something that should be brought up on the phone. I needed to tell him face to face.

I felt immense relief when I heard his car pulling up. I was always a little excited to hear it, but this time it felt like a weight had just lifted from my shoulders. I almost tripped running down the stairs to the door to greet him. I'm still not sure why I grabbed onto the handrail to save myself a hefty tumble that might have given me the miscarriage to solve my new problem, but no, I was already in the mindset of saving this baby at all cost. I really don't know where that came from.

Why would I want to bring a baby into this slow descent to hell? Where did this strange maternal instinct come from when my old plan was to just palm off my children to Jackie, a thought I now considered preposterous? Not just because we were no longer friends, but also as I now felt this absurd need for this child to be mine. Someone for me to love and protect above all else. Where did these odd feelings come from?

000-09-000

A S I OPENED THE door to see Michael in the distance, slowly getting out of his car, I noticed a flash of neon on his hand. Michael had taken the mark. So many thoughts rushed through my mind as he walked slowly towards me. Was I angry, disappointed, surprised? Then strangely enough I had a sense of relief. Michael had done the right thing. Again, he had appeared just in time to save us and our new child from the horrors that were awaiting those who were still unmarked. I would now be safe from the big bad world, hiding out in my beautiful mansion with my soon-to-be child.

Despite all the strange things that I had seen, I still didn't truly think that Michael having the mark meant he was now destined for hell. I actually didn't even care because I still couldn't believe that a book had really created the problem. I was fairly certain that mankind had. Why, I would probably never know, but originally there was great profit made by some. I had to assume it was started by that human desire for power and money, possibly without thought of the monster they were about to create or just not caring because they would have already made their money.

Michael was certainly going to be our saviour. I knew the time was quickly approaching when online ordering was going to be impossible without that mark; we had already been sent a scanner.

I was feeling that this turn of events had given me a great advantage. I would still be able to watch the planet's demise from my unmarked perspective while having Michael's new assessment and attitude of how the marked saw our evolving future, and I'd still be able to eat – a really great bonus.

Positioning his powerful, now-marked hand on my shoulder, he sent excited shivers down my spine before he spoke in a tone that turned good feelings into uneasy shudders.

"We need to talk."

"Yeah, I can see that," I replied with a smile, trying to lighten what was feeling like a bad situation.

"You've got two days to leave this house," he said, as he handed me a card. "It's a place for people like you. You'll be safe there. And take your old car. You've already nearly cost me everything with your stupid beliefs. You're not getting the car as well. Actually, pack up your stuff and leave now! I can't believe the crap you've made me suffer for this long already." He handed me my old car keys and waved me along like a dog in his way. "Go, shoo, I'll wait out here while you get your stuff out of the house." He looked down at his watch. "Hurry! You've got fifteen minutes to get the hell out of here."

I said nothing as shock took over my body and I found it very difficult to actually move. The man I worshipped had just sent me into a frozen state of fear and had I been able to speak, 'What the fuck?' would have been the only words I could have uttered.

He seemed awfully serious, so I had to use all my strength to make my legs move so that I could at least retrieve my clothes. I quickly built up enough anger for my blood to boil and thaw out my body but it still wasn't enough heat to get any words from my mouth. As I scurried through the house, desperately trying to find everything that belonged to me, I prayed that this was all some sort of giant prank. I hoped that as I appeared from the house, there would be Michael, his arms open to embrace me and that smile I once loved so much telling me that he was only joking. It wasn't the case. He stood in the doorway, arms crossed and a face filled with hate.

"You got five minutes to get off this property."

Should I have told him that I was carrying his baby? I'll never know because my vocal chords were still frozen in fear, and if it wasn't that, it was anger that I felt he now had no right to know that I was carrying his unborn child. He'd jumped from hero to zero, and I was too hurt and mystified by his behaviour to let out a single word. I also felt that I had to get to my car quickly because I really don't know what would have happened if I didn't make it in his fifteen minutes and I certainly didn't have the courage to find out.

I now understood the fear of women living with domestic violence. I'd always wondered why they didn't just fight back or leave the men that were causing them so much pain. Even though he never actually touched me, I felt I was now one of them in a way. How horrendous would it be for someone to be beaten by the person that they thought they loved when I couldn't even cope with being spoken badly to?

The relief I felt when I left that driveway I had once been so attached to left me feeling even more confused. I felt like I had just escaped from some demon that had overtaken my true love. Thinking back, he could have been a lot meaner had that mark really possessed his soul as I had now decided it had. I would have thought that rather than just giving me time to leave he might have suggested that I too get the mark or anything other than what transpired.

Even my friends were nicer to me when they first received the mark and I certainly hadn't been intimate with any of them, so Michael's abrupt turnaround was something I was never going to comprehend. Having my old car filled with CDs, I let the tears flood from my face with every sad song I could muster. When I accidently chose a positive track, it helped me to try to get a grip on my situation. My love, my life, was now all gone but I had something new that had to be protected so there was no time to wallow in self-pity. I had to drive to this address that Michael had so politely shoved into my hand.

I had heard of these places where the unmarked could now go to be safe and protected, and with a baby on the way I really had no other choice. The tears and self-pity never really subsided. I was alone and heading to possibly some hippy-type commune with no money and probably just enough fuel to get me there.

I wanted so badly to return to my parents, but I knew that their rejection in person again would be more than I could cope with. I glanced down at my phone for the direction I needed to follow to my unknown destination and decided that perhaps a quick phone call to my mother was worth a shot. Maybe if I told her of my unenviable situation and the fact that I was carrying her grandchild, she might take me back like a parent used to before all this mess started, but there was no longer service on my phone. Somehow Michael had managed to cut off my phone. I didn't have the fuel to drive back to my parents so a call had been my only hope.

Should I just turn around and beg Michael's forgiveness for whatever it was that I had done? Tell him that I was carrying his child and swallow my pride or whatever it was that had deterred me from receiving the mark? That was probably the cleverer option, but I no longer had the fuel to return. There was no point dwelling on the fact that it was no longer viable to turn back because there was obviously some deeper reason that I hadn't thought of it earlier, and I was never going to know why that was.

With the red glow of dusk encompassing the miles of barren farmland I was driving through, I felt like I was trapped in a horror movie. I could feel myself abusing this moron on the television, telling her to turn back, pointing out her obvious stupidity in driving along such a desolate road alone where the only possible outcome was the Bates Motel or worse.

I'm not sure if it really looked as scary as I had worked it up to be. I knew if I had been on a road trip with Michael I would consider the orange hue covering the land to be quite magnificent and worth a photo stop. Then I wouldn't have been travelling to a scary unknown future like I was now. It was amazing how the one image could conjure up two completely opposite feelings. Even stranger was that this irrelevant rubbish was rushing through my head at all. I put it down to fear or the ramblings of someone that anxiety was now sending insane.

All of a sudden, in the fading light I noticed a tall, attractive fence that seemed to go on as far the eye could see. It reminded me of the magnificent property I had just been thrown out of but on a much larger scale. An avenue of gigantic trees formed perfect lines above the neatly rendered, white wall.

For at least forty minutes I drove beside the massive construction with my fuel light flashing and beeping, desperately trying to tell myself the end was near. When I finally arrived at what looked like the pearly gates of heaven, the beeping and flashing stopped – fortunately, my car didn't. As the mysterious gates opened for me, I was able to calmly drive straight into what I now believed may have been heaven.

As I pulled up alongside a building that looked like it had been replanted from the Vegas strip, I was calmly ushered from my automobile and taken inside. My keys were gently taken from me, then I was quickly scanned and fingerprinted for what the well-dressed staff explained were security reasons. I was expecting to hear the dinging of poker machines but instead the sound of tasteful elevator music actually soothed the ears. I truly began feeling that I had really arrived in some safe, peaceful paradise, but the glowing mark on everyone's hand reminded me of the predicament I was in.

They were all extremely obliging but the sense that it was all a bit of an act crept through, with their eagerness to please barely hiding the gritted teeth. I was taken to a luxurious couch and offered a welcome drink, service that I'd always assumed Michael and I may have received, had we ever been able to travel to those luxury destinations we had dreamed about.

"So do you need my name and details?" I asked the man offering me a drink.

"No need," he replied, "Just sit back and relax. When all your belongings have been collected from your car, we'll take you and them to your apartment."

"Ok." That's all I had, but I don't think he was really waiting for a clever comeback anyway. He didn't show any indication of wanting to spend any quality time with me, just get the job done and back away quickly. Conversation was not necessarily part of his job description.

I cautiously brought the lime-green cocktail to my lips and, like a professional wine taster, swished the liquid, gave it a light sniff and swallowed enough to barely dampen my teeth. I'm not sure what I expected this strange ritual to accomplish as I doubted it was going to have an obvious taste of poison. Even if it had, I was unsure what I could do to avoid the situation I was in. I could have avoided drinking poison but, if they wanted me dead, it was probably a better option. With that thought in mind I not only sculled the drink, I found the confidence to attract someone's attention and request another.

After waiting around for approximately two hours and consuming six potentially dangerous cocktails, a woman led me through the building, which was deceptively smaller than it had first appeared, took me outside and drove me to my apartment. It was a good ten minute drive, and although it was dark, the rows of small condominiums gave me the impression I had just arrived in a modern housing estate. I was taken by lift to my third-storey apartment where my belongings were waiting for me.

The apartment had beautiful, hardwood floors, showroom furniture, a small modern kitchen and a flat-screen television that I was informed had access to hundreds of channels. There was one ample bedroom, a bathroom with spa bath, a walk-in robe and a gorgeous little balcony that overlooked a large pool. I'd never holidayed in such nice accommodation, and these marked people who generally hated people like myself were letting us stay here free of charge. It was very odd.

"Who pays for all this?" I asked the woman that had brought me here.

"We do get some sizable donations from wealthy philanthropists," she answered. "This is a large agricultural undertaking that supplies fruit and vegetables to the outside world – an undertaking that pays considerably well since we have all now had vegetarianism thrust upon us by your lot." Her comment exposed her obvious resentment towards me and concluded her ability to continue forced pleasantries. "You can start working tomorrow. You'll be collected at nine."

With that she was gone. I might have cared had I not been preparing to snuggle under the covers and uncontrollably cry myself to sleep. I'm not convinced that I had always been one of those people consumed with self-pity, but I really felt that now I had more than enough reason to become one. They say it's better to have loved and lost than to never have loved at all. I'm tipping the person who first suggested that didn't even own a pet. It's absolute crap.

If you have something wonderful and lose it, then you know what you have lost. If you've never had anything or anyone amazing, you would never know what you're missing. That would have been a way better option, especially now I knew he was really gone forever. It was a stupid saying; it was wrong; and it turned out that I was much better at feeling sorry for myself than I could have ever imagined.

I woke quite early the next morning, possibly because of the surprisingly uncomfortable bed I was now destined to suffer. After a pitifully low water pressured shower, I realised that my new home was more of a mirage than the luxury apartment I thought I had entered the night before. Even through the tiny slits of vision through my heavily puffed up eyes, I could see how cheaply put together my new digs were.

Everything in the apartment was poorly thrown together: lots of plastic with lots of cheap throw rugs and rubber cushions giving a quick first impression of some type of quality, but it was all an illusion. Even the television displayed a picture quality so poor, it was almost painful on the eye to watch. There were many channels but they were full of re-runs and there was not one news station to be found. With no computer in sight I was beginning to realise that contact with the outside world was no longer an option.

The place was now feeling more like a prison than a sanctuary but I wasn't sure what I could do about it. I'd been willing to move to the country with Michael, and apart from his absence, this was probably a step-up. At least there were basic amenities like a flushing toilet and slightly running water. I remembered the pool I had seen from my balcony, so I quickly raced out to check it wasn't just a fish-pond.

The balcony could barely fit the rubbishy looking table and chair squished into the corner, but the pool looked even more attractive than I recalled. It was enormous: sparkling blue and surrounded by lovely sun lounges and palm trees. Like some magnificent oasis pulled directly from a luxury resort catalogue, it looked incredibly inviting.

I'd never been on a real holiday so I assumed that was possibly what the developers did, spend all their money on the outside and make the accommodation cheaply but pretty enough to take a good photo. My only travelling friend generally stayed in third-world jungles so my knowledge of these things was very limited.

The mysterious staff running this place had already unpacked my personal items. As I perused my neatly hung and colour-coded designer outfits, I noticed a large section of undesirable outfits that really didn't suit my wardrobe: very rustic looking shorts, shirts and the occasional pair of tracksuit pants – items I would never have considered even in my scariest nightmares. I noticed a pair of icky brown men's work boots that looked very much my size. Then I remembered I was going to have to work here, and my days of being a well-dressed showpiece were evaporating and I was turning into Farmer Joe.

Once it would have bothered me more but I realised that my appearance had been deteriorating since the mark first appeared. My hair and once regularly manicured nails had already suffered from extreme neglect. I had survived that, so I was just descending to that last step down the socially acceptable ladder of no return. Placing my shaky legs into the bargain-basement pair of tracksuit pants was actually a little liberating. I would no longer need to impress anyone. To be honest, these new unattractive clothes were so comfortable that I wished I'd had the courage to wear them before now.

Simone and I had constantly put Emily down for dressing inappropriately. She would often meet us for lunch in tracksuit pants and an old scruffy shirt. She ignored our judgmental attitudes and basically told us to get stuffed. Maybe that's what made her so strong; she was comfortable. I needed courage now more than ever before, so if I could gain some strength of character from my new attire, that's what I was going to do. Having Emily here with me would have been even better, but my memories of her were all that I had. So, clothes and the flashbacks of my amazing friend were going to get me through this new unknown with the courage and power that would have made her proud. That was to be my new plan and, if I failed, at least I would have done it in comfort.

A quick glance in the mirror proved to be quite the incentive, as I looked pretty darn good in my beyond-casual attire; comfortable and attractive, maybe this place was looking up, I thought. As I ventured from my unit, I was greeted by a group of like-dressed people: men and women all in my age group. Surrounded by identical white units as far as the eye could see, we all stood waiting, sharing quick pleasantries like the Good Morning fish tank scene in 'Monty Python's Meaning of Life'.

"Morning." "Morning." And on it went. The place looked like a cardboard backdrop from Universal Studios, and when the back-lot tour tram arrived, I actually slapped myself across the face to try and snap out of this altered reality.

"Did that to myself when I first arrived," commented an attractive dark-haired man – many of the others nodded in agreement. I followed them onto our lift, and once I sat down, I noticed that I could see nothing through the large glass side windows except my own reflection, which seemed to have lost its earlier attractiveness. Once on the tram we could no longer see outside, and the earlier smiles and greetings had become lost under a cone of silence. Everyone sat there without uttering a word, which was really creepy as the trip lasted a good hour.

Arriving at our destination where lines of fruit trees seemed to extend forever, the chatter returned as we all disembarked. The same attractive man that had spoken to me previously was now happy to converse again.

"Hi, I'm Timothy," he said, offering his hand. "The bus is bugged so we no longer speak during the trip. There was a couple who complained on the trip about the conditions and we never saw them again."

"Where did they go?" I asked, knowing it was probably a stupid question.

"Not a clue, but as things are so strange around here, we all decided that it was safer to assume that they went nowhere better. For safety we all talk to each other here or by the pool because nothing said in those two places has ever had any repercussions."

"Ok, I'm Elisha." I thought I better tell him my name. "Has anyone ever thought about just leaving here?"

"For a start nobody knows how, and any people who have been known to want to leave have supposedly mentioned it in their units and, like the couple on the tram, disappeared soon after."

"So we are truly in a prison?" I asked, becoming incredibly scared of my new situation.

"No, it's not that bad," Timothy replied with a slight smile. "We pick fruit five days a week, and it seems to be irrelevant how well we work. We are incredibly well looked after with a never-ending supply of food, and our weekends are spent lazing around the pool or entertaining ourselves in games rooms, with everything from bowling to pinball machines. Behind that we have basketball, tennis courts, a large oval and a gym. It beats the hell out of sleeping under bridges and rummaging through garbage bins for a meal. That's all there is for us on the outside, so why would we want to leave?"

"Why are there no elderly or children around?" I asked, beginning to worry about my unborn child.

"I assume the elderly are kept in a retirement part of the complex. A lot of children are born, but when the women go into labour they are whisked away with their husbands. They turn up quite contented a few months later without the child because they are put into some sort of day care centre and the parents join them on the weekends."

"So parenthood without the responsibility?" I asked, a little confused by his whatever attitude. "You don't think that's a bit strange. I'd like to see my child more than two days a week."

"I can only tell you what I see. They are probably just happy that they are able to give birth with some medical assistance and have their children well fed and educated – an option no longer possible outside of these walls."

He had a very good point but I'm not sure I wanted to be separated from my child when I had never had to suffer the hardships that most of these people had obviously endured. Somewhere beyond these walls I had once had family and a wonderful fiancé, and

I was now willing to take that mark and fight my way back into their lives.

"So who can I speak to about getting the mark and going home?" I asked.

"No-one," he answered, seeming a little uneasy that I would even ask that. "The marked no longer associate with us at all. Didn't you notice the bus driver was in a separate carriage, completely covered in thick glass, so you won't get any response from him. He is the only one you will even see with the mark. They fill our cupboards and fridges while we are out here, lay our lunch out here before we arrive. They try to avoid us at all costs, and those that have had the opportunity to ask about the mark have been given a very firm straight out no.

"There is no point trying to fight them on it because if you do see someone with the mark, you will notice that they are always carrying a weapon and they give the impression they wouldn't hesitate to use it. Don't stress. In a week or two you'll learn to enjoy this place and maybe even hook up with one of the many attractive men poolside on the weekend. If you're really desperate, I'm available."

I didn't see that coming so I just gave him a slightly shocked grin. I was far from over Michael but if I was going to be stuck here forever, I certainly wasn't ruling it out.

It seemed Timothy had been correct. The work had been incredibly easy and, as we were under no pressure, I think we actually picked more fruit. By two thirty when our lift home would arrive, the bins would be overflowing. If someone was injured on the job or by the pool, a team of masked, hazmat-suited medical personnel would arrive and either treat the victim on the spot or whisk them off and return them when they were healed. It was like a scene from an Ebola breakout, with us being the highly contagious population they needed to be protected from. Those who'd been hospitalised returned with the same stories of being treated by fully suited medical practitioners.

I'm not sure if we were all harbouring some contagion or if it was just the easiest way to keep some sort of distance between them and us. They would only answer questions relating directly to the incident – anything else would be completely ignored. I once thought of asking a team of them about where I could go to receive the mark but I couldn't work up the courage or remove my fear of what unknown consequence might result from my question. So, like everybody else, I just sat back in my deckchair, watching the marked efficiently treat the patient and disappear without a trace.

I often wished that Emily could have been here with me. Michael's attitude had left such a bitter taste I was glad of his absence. I decided to take Timothy's advice and make the most of my strange situation and his offer of a sexual encounter more than once. It seemed that the gym and swimming pool were like a meat market of fairly fit and healthy bodies. Being subjected to half-naked members of the opposite sex so consistently would have made even the most frigid person horny.

Our lives consisted of work, re-runs, sporting activities or sex, so we constantly participated in them all. It had been the first time that I had sat and talked with a group of people where one wasn't playing with their smart phone. I would have thought that would have been a bonus until I realised that when a contentious subject arrived none of us could google it. Arguments could no longer be settled with a few clicks, and those easy answers to irrelevant questions we'd forgotten were no longer available. I don't think even Emily would have enjoyed this internet-free world. There's nothing worse than losing something that you had learnt to be so dependent on.

There were no future dreams or aspirations to occupy our minds, no contact or even knowledge of the outside world. We did have access to reading material in the form of us each being left with a tablet full of thousands of books that they had obviously chosen and the standard games of solitaire and free cell. But there was no access to the web or reading material of any sort that could make one feel the need to question anything. It was as if I had been forced to join some obscure cult, cut off from the real world and forced to live in some alternative reality.

To be honest, this life should have suited me perfectly as I was generally someone who didn't question anything much or have much thought about the future. Like most of the residents of my new home, I had already slept with half the eligible men and I really missed shopping. I had not been able to appease my habit for a long time anyway as I had been unable to walk into a store without the mark, and to be honest, there weren't many stores left. Giant companies had bought out the smaller ones leaving us with the choice of giant warehouse-type buildings, selling everything from toothpaste to angle grinders all under the store's home brand. Choice and competition had been taken away, making my lack of having the mark fairly irrelevant to my shopping obsession on the outside world.

Like many of the women in our group, my stomach was beginning to grow. With the sexfest going on and no available contraception, pregnancy was naturally a regular occurrence. Unlike myself, most of the women were expecting multiple births, making one wonder what strange additives were being introduced to our food.

I had become pregnant on the outside; most of the women had been impregnated here. I'm not sure how they could have worked out the father but I don't think that they cared. I began to wonder why they would be encouraging us to breed at all, let alone in multiples. I had begun questioning things again. What was wrong with me? Why couldn't I just go back to my ways before the mark? Where had this strange new me come from, and how much more trouble was it going to get me into?

The other women I spoke to were more than happy with their situation and I annoyed them even suggesting the inconsistencies that I'd identified. I was supposedly with my own kind, yet again I felt so alone.

As my stomach increased, so did my uneasy feeling about my situation. I began watching the others, laughing and enjoying their surroundings. They seemed to have no concerns about their future and reminded me of a group of happy, mindless drones. I probably used to look that way to my friends except Simone; her carefree attitude even annoyed me at times. I was seriously becoming Emily, first with the mark and now actually paying attention to things that I now found quite unrealistic. I tried so hard to just sit back and enjoy, but I could no longer stop myself from trying to find the answers to the many questions that now kept me awake every night.

What was this place? Why were we being so well looked after when I knew many marked people were suffering in the real world? How could I cope with only seeing my child on the weekends? What were they doing to these children? What were their plans for us? Why did no-one else share in my thirst for answers? Why did I care?

There was no reason for me to care. Nobody else did and most of them had been here much longer than me. I really hated this irresistible urge to understand my situation, but I found myself desperately needing to have my questions answered.

That need was becoming more than I could contain and my child's arrival date was fast approaching. They would soon arrive in their biohazard outfits to take me away, so time was no longer on my side. I also found it very strange that I was so affected by this approaching baby. The fact that I would be free here to leave child-raising to others should have been a perfect scenario. I had always said I intended to pass my offspring onto Jackie. What was with this extreme affection to my unborn child?

I don't know if it was my situation that caused it or if this was just what happened to people when they found out they were soon to be responsible for another human life. I truly believe it was the second because just knowing I had a living thing in my stomach gave me the immediate feeling of duty to protect it, and I felt that getting it away from here was the only way to do so. I intended to find a way to leave this perfectly safe haven with my innocent child, and I really didn't know why I was even considering it.

The chance of my friends and family taking me back were slim. I had never managed to obtain the life supply of canned goods and camping equipment that could have helped me to survive out in the real world, so I wasn't sure what I could really accomplish by leaving. Even if I had been blessed with fishing or hunting skills, there was nothing left outside to catch. It was a bold move, wanting to leave with no real knowledge of how to do it. My stupidity had already got me this far so it wasn't going to let me just stop here.

Against better judgment that I was now lacking, I carefully began to put my escape plan into action. My intentions were now to find a way to quietly break out, get myself the mark and pray that if Michael would not take me back, maybe my parents or friends would. I'd seen plenty of films where the hero made some great escape but unfortunately I couldn't remember any of them, and naturally there was no such type of show on the thousands of re-runs that I now had access to.

I had to figure this out alone – a very undesirable situation for someone who'd never really done anything without the help of others. Even my employment came about through a family friend – I didn't even have a resume. My emails, Facebook page, Twitter account, everything set up by friends. Until I arrived here, leaving me many private moments to think, I had no idea of how useless I really was, and now realising my deficiencies, I was intending to flee the impenetrable.

I was one seriously lost soul, but I cleverly used the realisation of my pointlessness to slightly take away my fear. What did I have to lose? I had done nothing of worth my entire life so I wasn't going to make much of a mother anyway. If I failed and they knocked me off, no-one was ever going to care anyway. I had a lot of time for self-pity but this time I was actually going to use it for good.

I began by paying much more attention to my surroundings and asking innocent questions while lazing around the pool and working. My trip to the gym had really excited me when I noticed there were pushbikes. They were neatly stacked outside the back of the gymnasium with no locks or obvious cameras looking down at them, and they conveniently led to a cemented path that surrounded the large oval. Behind the oval was a forest of unkempt trees with no sign of a fence, which seemed odd in anotherwise highly guarded place.

First, I had to worry about the fact that they were racing bikes with that evil middle bar. I'd always wondered why men's bikes had a bar when they were so much more protective of their crutch than we were. I wasn't much of a cyclist to start with, now I needed to relearn on a horrible bike with a getting-larger-by-the-day stomach. But learn I did, before and after work everyday, I just explained to everyone that I felt the need to get fit for my new baby. They actually believed me.

I quickly learnt from my many spills that they didn't seem to be watching over the oval or bike track. I even tested them a couple of times when there was no-one else around by intentionally falling off and lying on the ground for a long time pretending to hold my stomach in pain. When the outbreak squad did not arrive, I knew they obviously couldn't see me. There was a fence, well hidden in the trees, but it seemed to be made from thin wire and I could see large gaps under it. A pair of old heels was the best I could come up with for a shovel. As I explained before, this was not my forte. I decided that I had found my escape route and I just needed the right conditions to attempt it.

When an unusually rainy afternoon arrived, I knew it was my time to put my plan into action, especially since the arrival of my child was becoming obviously closer. I was very fortunate that I seemed to be carrying my baby quite well. I noticed other women with stomachs twice the size of mine, and they had not been pregnant for nearly as long. I felt a little overcome with sadness as I disembarked the tram for what I hoped to be the last time. Although I never felt close to any of these people, they were the closest things to friends that I now had. Almost blowing my cover, I gave Timothy a light hug and I just explained it away as hormonal emotions when I noticed the confusion in his smile. My excuse worked so well I realised I could have blamed any of my strange behaviour on it.

From my balcony the wet pool area with its dripping umbrellas looked completely desolate. I grabbed a pair of picking gloves and shoved my lonesome high heel down my top, a favourite hoodie I had stolen from Michael during my eviction from his palace, my tiny bit of payback. My head and hands nicely covered, I walked towards the back of the gym with conviction.

As I'd become such an avid cyclist, no-one was likely to question my behaviour. I now more professionally boarded my chosen bike and rode away to put my plan in motion. Although there were many serious riders in our group who wouldn't have cared about the weather, they were the spandex-wearing type so I had a good ten to twenty minutes up my sleeve.

Undetected I powered towards the coverage of trees. It wasn't long before I had to dismount my ride as it wasn't really suited to the now-rugged terrain. A BMX would have been a much better option and much easier to lug around. The bike did not appreciate my treatment of it but I assumed I was in an extremely large fortress that would have been too hard to escape from by foot. If I did get out, I knew that it had been an awfully long drive to get here, so civilisation was going to take a long ride to find.

The fence's lack of maintenance was even better than I had expected. My shoe had been an unnecessary addition but one that I was happy to uncomfortably keep. Apart from the crown of thorns

I received as the wire displaced my hoodie, cutting my forehead to shreds, the bike only caused a few backward stumbles as it was thinner than myself. It would have been the most entertaining YouTube download, and who knew, maybe it was.

It seemed a little too easy to get this far so it did cross my mind it was some kind of set up to entertain those marked monsters. They hated us before so there had to be some underhanded reason for them looking after us so well now. Funniest home videos could have been the answer. I doubted it, but there was nothing else to explain it.

My exploits so far had taken a great deal longer than I expected as I noticed the sun disappearing through the small gaps of the canopy. I was now trekking through a creepy forest using my bike to guide me from smacking into tree stumps. I almost wished for a rustle or the spine-chilling hoot of an owl, but knew they were sounds my child was never going to hear. Wildlife was now history. Maybe this wasn't a world that I wanted to bring an innocent baby into. It was too late now and the sharp pains now tearing through my stomach reminded me of how much trouble I was really in.

In the distance I noticed a lighter shade of black and presumed it had to be my way out of the forest so I sped up, causing branches to find their way through my clothes and rip into any skin they found available. Doubling over in pain every few minutes, I could hear the blood drops crackle onto the leaves below in the silence and knew my wounds were more serious than I had envisaged. The beauty was that labour pains had completely wiped any thought of those annoying little scratches that before I would have considered unbearable.

I never realised how thick bushes became when no-one bothered clearing the undergrowth. And why, in a place like this, would they let the shrub become so out of control? The many thorny plants were probably left to stop others like myself trying to make their escape, but if I could manage the many abrasions I had encountered, I couldn't imagine there would be much weaker than me being turned off their attempt. Maybe it was left like this to fool us into thinking we really were making the perfect escape into the wilderness. But if I wasn't dopey enough to believe that, I doubt anyone else would have been.

I eventually emerged from the bushes to find myself on a darkened road. The other side seemed to be a continuation of the forest I had just left. I glanced to my right, more forest. To my left and across the road was the source of light I had been heading towards – a series of dimly lit, white concrete structures that looked old and dirty and reminded me of the buildings that used to make me shiver when we drove past as a child. I'm not sure why I didn't just cross over to the next forest but this insane, new me decided to approach the buildings instead. Like a mosquito flying into a bug zapper, I was hypnotised by the light and began to ride towards it on my now very wobbly bike.

000-10-000

THE FIRST BUILDING, ALTHOUGH not made of tin, reminded me of a shed that friends of the family used to house their poultry on their farm, except this one was huge, with lots of windows and massive locks on its front entry. Although barbed wire surrounded the window, I knew that I had to find away to peek inside. I'd been cut to shreds anyway. What were a few more scratches in the grand scheme of things? So, I wheeled my shaky bike and forced it into the barbed wire fence near what looked to be a broken window well above my head height. Being born with no great agility to begin with, handicapped by a large protruding stomach and with a barbed wire fence as leverage, against all odds I managed to wrench myself up onto my bicycle seat.

I slowly peered into what looked like a dimly lit bomb shelter full of people. Army-barracks bunk beds lined up against the walls on both sides as far as I could see. In the middle some fold-up tables overflowed with food, while others were covered with sets of cards and board games. Smaller card tables were dotted throughout with people sitting around them on fold-up chairs. Some were playing cards, others perusing the same tablets that I'd had in my apartment. The majority of the people were not young, so I now had an idea of where the missing oldies were hanging out, but I noticed a lot of children too, people my age, and the occasional teenager.

Although it was difficult to get a clear view I noticed that some of the children seemed to be disabled in some way. They all seemed quite content and I noticed a lot of children's toys scattered around. The adults and teenagers were all helping out the children, chatting away with each other and, at another table, a group of middle-aged men were obviously having a wonderful game of poker as their laughter echoed throughout.

From my extremely uncomfortable vantage point I couldn't understand why they were all so happy because it looked like a prison camp to me, or more so, like an emergency shelter set up after a disaster. The food looked good and there seemed to be a never-ending supply of drinks. The laughing men looked and behaved as though they were drinking alcohol – something the fruit pickers' quarters were seriously lacking.

Some of the older women were happily reading stories to the young children like teachers in a classroom. Some looked mesmerised by the women's stories being told with more creativity than I remembered teachers displaying, while some were completely disinterested and just annoying the others. That behaviour I did remember but these children seemed a little more uncontrollable than I remembered. The bad ones were behaving like children that desperately needed a smack, and they were missing that cuteness that would generally stop you enforcing the punishment. Of course, having what looked like the sweetest of grandmothers looking after them, I realised discipline was probably never going to be enforced in this place.

Overall everyone seemed to be enjoying themselves and were completely unaware of the bad behaviour, so it really didn't matter. Older men were playing board games with each other, reminding me of the old days, seeing chess boards in the park. Perhaps this was just a temporary place to accommodate people while they were waiting for better accommodation. I had noticed that our section seemed to be quite full.

After living on the streets in the outside world, raiding bins for food, they probably considered this place a palace. They certainly didn't look emaciated. Many of them looked incredibly well fed and, by the quality and quantity of the food, I could see there was no reason for them not to be a bit chubby.

The marked were probably using this area to build them up so when they were released into the community, they would be able to work like us. What was I thinking – 'community'? Like I had just escaped from some normal place!

Watching this happiness and distorted normality had begun to cloud my judgment if I was starting to think what I was seeing was natural. There was nothing even slightly regular about having hundreds of people locked up in a ginormous shed. There was nothing right with any of this situation. I knew I needed to keep searching for answers and I wasn't going to get them here. No, I really had to escape but my subconscious kept ruining that idea so, with my bike and now bloodier hands, off I went to search the next building.

Why didn't I have this thirst for knowledge as a child at school and been able to use it for things to enhance my life? Not be consumed by it in a place where the answers I was seeking were going to do nothing for me except possibly endanger myself and my child. I wasn't actually controlling myself and my choices and I hadn't been for a while so there was no real point procrastinating, so off I went again looking for something I possibly didn't want to find.

Arriving close to the building I noticed a crushed rock parking bay. Beside it were about a dozen cars with a small old-fashioned streetlight casting a shadow over them. Luckily for me the woods were close and encroaching on the surprisingly long building, giving me good hidden vantage points. I still don't know why I wanted a better look but my labour pains had subsided so again I'd sort of forgotten that my original plan was just to escape. My curiosity intensified when I recognised the man making his way over to the dimly lit lamp.

It was Bradley, wearing a similar outfit to mine, talking on his mobile phone with a cigarette hanging from his lips. It was the smoke that really surprised me, as he was one of those holier than thou, rude, cough, cough someone is smoking near me non-smokers. There he was drawing back deeply on something he despised. I knew that he had lost his job but lowering himself to such an unenviable new wardrobe seemed completely out of character. He disappeared as quickly as he had arrived, but I noticed that he had left his phone behind next to the overflowing ashtray set up on a small table under the light.

Originally, I think my compulsion to take his phone came from some unrealistic thought that I may have been able to phone Michael, or even Simone, whom Bradley had just been on the phone to. What caused me instead to try to sneak a look inside the huge building, I doubt I will ever understand. I knew logically that making a phone call would be risky, yet logic played no role in stopping me from entering a potentially more dangerous building.

The door had been left wide open so I was able to sneak my way in undetected. Although very poorly lit, I could see that it looked like a giant desolate warehouse with its floors covered in dirt. Kicking the ground a little, I realised it was only soil. I could see doors in the distance but I knew that walking through them was not really an option if I was going to remain unnoticed. Shaking nervously at the thought of someone appearing from one of the doors, I quickly scanned the room for options.

I noticed an elevated steel walkway. It was incredibly high and obviously not recently used as its ladder was missing some rungs. A sane person would never have chosen to attempt such a dangerous feat but I hadn't been that for a while, so up I went. Initially I felt confident I could easily bypass the occasional missing rung, but as I arrived near the top, the three missing ones became a much larger problem.

The platform was just out of my reach but I could touch it with the tips of my fingers, which only made it more frustrating. My only option was to somehow grow a few more inches or try to jump while still using my other hand to hold onto the side rail. A risk that I probably wouldn't have cared about in my younger days of tree climbing, but I doubt I'd ever made it this high up a tree, and I now had a much larger stomach than back then. If I missed gripping onto the side bar of the walkway, I would have slipped and died, and that thought is what propelled me to try it. My lack of any real future was the reason behind this great excursion so stay here or die both shared the same appeal.

So I did it. I grabbed that side rail with such grace that I pulled myself onto the walkway without even scratching my oversized belly. I had a wonderful feeling of accomplishment, something that had been missing during my stay here. With no thought of a future, even when I had done something to be proud of, like fill my bucket before someone else or pass a good cyclist on the bike track, it didn't really matter. None of us really cared about anything anymore. I hadn't realised that until I was reminded of how doing something worthy used to feel.

So there I stood, hopefully well out of sight. As I was incredibly high I felt that as long as I was quiet, no-one would bother looking and then spotting me. The walkway, like so many things in this place, seemed to go on forever and I noticed that it was higher than the many pop-up walls ahead. Chances were that if I followed it, I would be able to see the complete layout of this strange place. I was also in luck as the rooms were lit with old pendant lights, keeping my vantage point in complete darkness. Even if someone had looked up, they would have found it difficult to see me. Inspired by the many horror films I had seen, I turned off the sound of Bradley's stolen phone, something that again encouraged me to feel proud at my own cleverness.

Quietly walking past many poorly lit, empty rooms, I began to feel that this had been a pointless expedition and since I had no idea why I had bothered to do it anyway, I was really regretting the fact that I wasn't in the woods trying to leave. Then I began hearing muffled screams that sent shivers throughout every part of my body. I had never heard anything like it before. I didn't know why it made me so uneasy, but I knew I never wanted to hear it again. Again I could not explain what drove me towards it, while every responsible emotion warned me against it.

Still dimly lit, the next room I looked down on was unfortunately not empty. It was filled with large, rusted cattle-loading ramps and surrounded by armed marked men with cattle prods, pitch forks and machetes. Not able to comprehend what I was seeing, for a split second I thought that these people had found a way to breed animals again.

Then my mind finally accepted what my eyes were seeing. Naked people were being prodded through the bars. I still can't explain how I was able to control the nausea or how I remained silent, but I did. I quickly ripped out Bradley's phone, my hands shaking as they had when I discovered my dead friend, and began filming the atrocities that I was trying not to see.

From the elderly down to children, the long line of people with fear in their eyes was beyond anything I could ever have imagined. Their hands were tied behind their backs and their mouths gagged to lessen the noise I assumed. The marked men, who seemed to be enjoying their job, were fiercely prodding them with pitchforks. I had always tried to believe that animals would never have been treated in this manner, but I was now feeling that it hadn't been the case.

The naked victims were being forced to walk towards a curtained-off area where the muffled screams were coming from. An ocean of tears were flowing from many as they cowered in vain to slow down the moving line, but they would just receive violent machete wounds from the marked men.

One fit looking man, possibly in his forties, began cautiously scanning the area around him. He had to know there was no possible escape. Maybe he was just hoping that they would shoot him, a far better option than what lay ahead. As one of the marked came within reach, somehow removing his wrist restraints, he threw his arms through the metal bars seizing the guard and smashing him firmly into the cage, causing his head to crack as he fell to the ground. Within seconds other marked men grabbed the man through the bars. One held him in a tight headlock, while the others tortured him slowly, slashing his achilles, his genitals and almost every other possible sensitive part of the human body. The guard he had attacked was obviously not too injured as he quickly joined in with his friends.

They made the other captives walk past him so as to make him suffer for the longest time possible, while making sure everyone noticed the punishment for insubordination. This once strong man had become a cowering grey shadow, showing no real signs of the vibrant human he must have once been. Although he now gave the impression of an empty shell, you could still faintly see the light of a tortured soul in his eyes.

It was the first time I had really truly noticed the difference. There was no light in these marked people's eyes. Possibly it was just these murderers suffering this affliction. I wished I had paid more attention to the many I had come across before. As I scoured the eyes of their captives, a light shone bright through the pain and tears. Were they and myself the only humans still filled with a soul? Did that mark really take everyone else's away? From where I was now standing, it seemed like a fairly safe bet. Even after they had completely butchered the man who had tried to defy them, they continued to taunt and punish anyone else that even glanced their way.

Many of the older men and women in line who had witnessed the man's torment stood tall and proud and fearlessly marched towards their certain doom. They did not look at their captors, just powered purposefully to their demise. It seemed to calm those around them and frustrate the marked men who were losing their excuses to continue their torture. I almost felt the urge to cheer their success until I remembered that I was not watching a film, and their moral victory was completely irrelevant to their terminal situation. No hero or earthly catastrophe was going to save them. They knew they were going to die and so did I. These humans were destined to the same fate as cattle in an abattoir. Even though I was probably doomed to join them, I still could not imagine what they must have been feeling. They were enduring hell on Earth and had to have been praying for some faint hope of a heavenly afterlife.

Just knowing that I could do nothing to save them was tearing through my insides. So how were there others able and willing to physically perpetrate it? All those horror stories of incomprehensible human behaviour were no longer a television program. I was now watching the suffering directly, with no conceivable reason for it happening. All I could think was that the overseers really had been possessed for them to behave so inhumanely.

When did the human race lose its ability to distinguish right from so unbelievably wrong? On deeper thought it had been done before. We had seen the horror of the Holocaust and atrocities in Cambodia, Rwanda and the Middle East, but this may have rivalled them. The thought of demonic possession seemed plausible but the answer never really came as to why.

Although repulsed beyond belief, I knew I had the ability to see what was happening behind that curtain. I really didn't want to, but the choice was no longer mine. I'd already seen too much and whatever steered me this far was again forcing me to complete what

I'd begun. I needed to film this, so beyond the curtain I ventured with less fear than I had anticipated.

What I had just seen had prepared me for the inconceivable – these people were being slaughtered. It was a sea of red, walls splattered in more blood than anyone could ever imagine. It seemed that there was a hell and I had just entered it. Frozen to the walkway, I watched an elderly gentleman who epitomised a loving grandfather, his head held high, walking straight and tall to the blood smeared man putting the bolt to his head as another clamped chains around his feet. Proving that my long-standing reservations about Bradley were correct, his new employment was triggering the stun gun that shocked these victims. He looked straight into the desperate eyes of his elderly victim without showing the slightest sign of emotion, then shoved him over to an oversized, heavily tattooed monster who slit the old man's throat with a grin, laughing as he revelled in his job.

"Aged meat coming," the monster yelled, to whom I don't know, then another flicked the switch to hang the carcass upside down and send the still-twitching victim along the conveyor. It was beyond horrendous but I knew that it was important to continue filming the not-so-cooperative child that followed him. Unfortunately closing my eyes didn't block my ears so I was still able to hear the killers and their insensitive banter.

"Nice bit of fresh young veal here. Dibs on taking this corpse home for dinner," laughed the throat-slitting monster before the child had even been zapped, making sure the child knew exactly what was to become of his body. Even Emily couldn't have envisioned this abhorrent end to civilisation. There were no words to describe the horror.

I'd always wondered why I didn't like Bradley but I could never have envisaged him sinking to this. Then again until now I could never have imagined any human capable of such horrendous behaviour. I'd heard of terrible things happening throughout the world but I felt this one was a whole new low that mankind really had no right to fall into.

To be honest, Bradley didn't seem to be relishing his job as much as the other marked psychopaths but he was still doing it so any mild feelings of pity for him were quickly diminished. I had a sufficient amount of video footage and I couldn't take the risk of being spotted and joining the line of annihilation. I just really didn't want to be there anymore. I backed away in complete silence, turned and walked at a speed I never thought possible. Approaching the ladder, giving no attention to the missing rungs, I basically slid to the ground within seconds.

Without turning once, I ran from the building, pulled my bike from the scrub and then collapsed remembering the happy people I had seen in the other building. They weren't waiting to go to a better place. They were being fattened up for slaughter. Having no idea what was awaiting them, they were enjoying themselves, thinking their lives had turned around for the better. They were in for one hell of an awakening so, even though I just desperately wanted to escape from this place, I knew that I had to try and warn them somehow. I couldn't be sure that even if they had the knowledge, there was anything they could do to stop it but I certainly had to give it a try.

Instead of returning to the scrub, I raced back to their building but with so much more at stake, I had trouble setting my bike up in the same position. I managed to block the returning labour pains with unbridled determination to get back up on that bike at all costs. I managed but I was not in the reasonably comfortable place that I had been earlier. After what I'd just seen I was never going to be again.

I gripped the barbed wire with my slaughtered hands, trying to pull myself up to warn these poor people. Finally, I could see into the building and, about to yell I'm not sure what, I noticed marked people entering the building. Dressed in their outbreak suits, they were delivering even more food. I didn't know how long they were going to be, and I really didn't want to stay and find out. I needed to leave but yelling out a warning was just a death warrant for myself so I had to find another way to let them know. I had Bradley's phone and a high-heel shoe, and the shoe really wasn't giving me any answers. I had to warn these people but I didn't know how. I knew the phone was the right thing to do but I just couldn't part with it.

Staring down at the potentially life-saving device, I noticed a tiny pen planted in its case. I became very excited until I realised there was no paper. I pulled out my overpriced, filthy shoe and through the never-ending stream of tears that flooded onto it, I noticed the sole was white leather.

In my precarious state, balancing on an unsteady bike, I soon decided that I had no other choice but to disembark. It felt as though that option was an unnecessary time-waster, but I needed two hands for the job so I had no choice. Using my oversized hoody, I cleaned the layers of dirt from my shoe and managed to write a message on the sole that I prayed would help them. The blood-stains would hopefully help its authenticity, as I really had no idea what I could write that they would believe to be true. I just kept it simple – with little room and a barely working pen I had no other choice: *You need to escape. These people are farming you for food. Please believe me I have seen it.* I doubted that it would work but it was the best I could do and, if just one of them was a little worried about their situation, this could inspire them to take action.

I'm not sure what they could do to escape the seemingly impenetrable complex but as a group they had more chance than me. I really hoped that I hadn't just prolonged their suffering. I needed to believe that I had done the right thing because it was all I had to offer them. Any slight possibility they may have had of escape was worth the risk. I considered joining them because I could properly inform them of what I had just witnessed and maybe that would improve my chances of leaving this abhorrent place. Then I reconsidered, as they possibly wouldn't believe a word I had to say – even I could barely comprehend what I had seen. I couldn't guarantee their support which made the whole idea way too risky.

After pulling myself back onto the bicycle seat, I noticed the marked suits beginning to leave. Now more worried for my own safety because I didn't know where they were going, I very quickly threw the shoe into the building. It belted an unimpressed teenager on the head, the perfect target I thought. As much as I wanted to be sure that he bothered to read it, I was too worried for my own safety and got the hell away from there.

I disappeared as far into the forest as I could before the labour pains and a tree branch slashing a deep wound into my side, stopped me in my tracks. The vomit I had earlier contained was now uncontrollably gushing from my lips. To top it all off I began to feel a wet sensation running down my inner thighs. This baby was coming so I just collapsed in a heap on the ground.

My pain started to ease for a second, giving me time to upload the horrendous footage I had just shot. I should have done it earlier and thrown the people my phone, but clear thinking under pressure was obviously another talent that I was lacking, and to be honest, selfishness was the true reason I couldn't part with it. Now it was out there for the world to see and I prayed, something I was doing a lot more of lately, that if there was just one genuine human being left out there to spot it before the marked managed to delete it, they could do something about it – maybe even in time to save those poor people I couldn't.

I also sent it to Simone and all of the contacts Bradley had in his phone, including Michael. I can't be sure they didn't already know what he was up to but maybe watching the footage would bring them back from the darkness they had all become a part of. No feeling human being could watch this footage and ignore it, I believed with all my heart, and there had to be a conscience in at least one of these people I used to consider my friends.

Again I felt that strange feeling of admiration for myself for a job well done. I was alone in a forest about to give birth to a child destined to die along with myself, and I was having a bizarre moment of pride that was just not right in any way, shape or form. So I did the only sensible thing a clear thinking human being in my position would. I closed my eyes in the hope that I would fall asleep and awake to this just being a horrific nightmare.

The first part I accomplished, but I was awoken by the touch of a marked hand. As it was still incredibly dark I wasn't sure the man leaning over me noticed or even slightly cared about the fear that would have been reflected in my eyes.

"It's alright. I'm not going to hurt you," he said calmly, as I took in the mark on his hand, "But at daybreak somebody else will."

"What are you talking about?" I asked, even though I knew. Then finding some Dutch courage I continued with a little more confidence. "I filmed everything and I sent it out for the world to see."

"Excellent, I wish I had thought of doing something so clever." He grabbed the phone from my hand and then began filming himself, holding his hand with mark in full view.

"The meat you are eating are humans," he began broadcasting to the web. "They are farming those without the mark and serving them up on your dinner plates, and occasionally adding those of us already marked when we do something against their wishes. You need to stop this. You need to stand up and fight them now PLEASE!" He continued to give details of our whereabouts and other sites that he knew of.

"They are actually killing us for food?" I asked, even though I already knew the answer.

"You're being bred for it. I'm sure you noticed that you weren't the only pregnant woman in your compound. The minute you arrived here when they scanned your body they were collecting evidence of your fertility. Man or women, they have the technology to understand if you're going to be a good breeder or not. If not, then straight to the slaughter you go. If you are, they'll keep you for a few years, get as many offspring as they can, then off to the slaughter."

"You have been part of this, knowing everything that's been going on. How? Did the mark really suck out your soul?"

"Look, I knew what was going on," he began trying to explain himself without as much regret as I would have expected. "You have to understand that people like you have been a stain on humanity. You made life impossible for everyone, relentlessly thieving our food and property, but causing the extinction of almost every species was more than even I could handle.

"We needed you gone so you couldn't cause any more trouble. This was the perfect solution. It would give us the meat you took away and keep you locked up so you could never harm us again. Great idea I thought, until the next phase, which is soon to be implemented. The men will just have their sperm extracted then be killed. The women will be artificially inseminated, and there will be no more of this hiding the truth from you all. No more pretending to educate your offspring, no more pools to upkeep or gyms and accommodation. You and your children will just be forced to breed and pick fruit until your turn at the abattoir, a more efficient and cost-effective program, they say. That's where I drew the line."

"My hero," I interrupted sarcastically.

"No seriously. I really don't see the need to make your food suffer. I tried in vain to make them reconsider their new plan but they wouldn't, so I threatened to expose what they were doing and now I'm stuck here, about to be hunted down when the sun rises."

"They're going to hunt you?" I asked quite confused. "So why don't you just escape and help me get out of here."

"There is no way out, trust me. I helped design this place and there is no possible exit. The trophy hunters are going to be awfully happy to find you here. They'll end up with three for the price of one."

"What are you talking about?" I asked

"No such thing as hunting anymore, as there are no animals left so we came up with this great idea of charging astronomical prices for game hunters to come here and hunt the unmarked. Of course, when we came up with the idea, I could never have conceived that I would become one of the victims."

"Isn't that the most amusing retribution I have ever come across? Suffer! So what – they put your head on a wall?"

"I don't know. They just take the carcass home," he said, with no real hint of the terror he should have been feeling. I almost considered running back to the killing room. At least I wasn't destined to be a trophy head there. Although I wasn't intending to ask what they did with the heads, I just hoped they were at least eating the brains so they would all have to suffer some form of mad-cow-like disease, which I'd heard happens from doing that. Mind you, I doubt that they could have become any more insane than what I had just witnessed.

I was now desperately praying for some way for this to end in a speedy, less bloodthirsty manner. If a meteor shower was considering bringing an end to planet Earth, it really needed to happen now. Why did natural disasters only happen at the most inconvenient times? We'd trashed the planet and it really needed to pay us back quickly, but no, it was going to drag out our suffering for a long time to come. The Bible somehow forgot to mention that mankind was planning a new era of cannibalism. Perhaps if that had been added in, people may have taken a little more notice. It crapped on about mythical beasts but nothing really warned us that most were going to become psychotic human-flesh-eating demon types. A heads up would have been appreciated since the writers obviously knew what was coming.

I didn't even have a weapon to nicely knock my child and myself off – the only time it had seemed like the most sensible option. My only hope now was that childbirth might kill us both, and I was seriously about to find out.

"So hunters are going to appear and shoot me and my newborn baby?" I asked, still shocked by my situation.

"Oh no," he answered. "They are only allowed to hunt in here with knives, occasionally machetes. Guns would make the whole experience a little too quick and sterile."

"Knowing all this, why don't you look as terrified as you should be?" I had to ask, even though every answer I had received so far was just making my situation more unbearable.

"I don't really know. Perhaps I don't believe that they will really kill me as I still have the mark, and that would be murder."

"But killing my newborn wouldn't?"

"It won't have been marked, so no," he replied in the matter-of-fact way he'd answered all of my previous questions. All the horror stories I had heard of what had been inflicted on so many over the years had obviously come back to one simple thing – anyone could be brainwashed into doing anything, no matter how against their original nature it was.

The superior race filled with infinite knowledge could be completely controlled with suggestion. No-one would save us from the horror awaiting us because they'd be programmed not to. No amount of pleading was going to turn them back in the limited amount of time we had left. All I could now hope for was a better afterlife for the two of us, praying some type of heaven really did exist. Funny how one finds the need to pray when they are confronted by their imminent end. I'm not sure that I had really become a believer. It was just desperation, hoping that there must be something greater elsewhere or what was the point of any of this.

With no chance of survival, I suggested the marked man should probably go away and leave me to suffer alone. I thought he must have thought there was some greater being that might forgive him if he helped me in my dire situation because he wouldn't leave. But no, he was staying so he could use me as his human shield – maybe buying time to bargain for his own life. He didn't want redemption because he didn't think for a moment that he needed it.

The sun was beginning to rise and the pain in my stomach was becoming so unbearable that I jerked my head back hard, slamming it into a tree.

I AWOKE IN A clean instrument-filled hospital room, screaming to see my child, and when no-one acknowledged my calls, I fell back asleep. The next time I awoke, I was surrounded by familiar faces – from my parents to the long-departed Emily. It was Emily, and I could not contain my excitement of seeing her alive, forgetting for a moment that I too was alive. It really had been a dream. All my prayers had been answered. I had conjured up the unthinkable, but it was alright because I was safe now, and the world I had just imagined was pretend. I was never going to waste one precious moment of the old world that I'd returned to.

I gave Emily the most affectionate hug I could muster, while giving no attention to either my parents or Simone and Jackie. They all looked surprised by my reaction but as it seemed that I had just awoken from a coma, they were willing to forgive my favouritism.

"They didn't know if you were ever going to wake up," said my mother with relief. "They have no idea why you were even in a coma," she continued. "It wasn't even a bad car accident and yet you've been asleep for over three years."

"That's right!" I began to remember the accident that occurred before my life turned into a trip to hell. "It was a flock of doves!" I exclaimed, now recalling the details. "They were flying straight into me, splattering all over the windscreen. I had to try to pull away to avoid them."

"No darling," said my mother, softly stroking my forehead like I was a two year old. "They found no evidence of any little birdies or anything."

If they didn't believe the doves, they were never going to accept the horror story that came after it, so I decided not to say another thing. I began to feel that maybe I had seen something that I couldn't really just explain away as a three year dream. I had also decided that Emily was the only person that I had any real chance of ever trusting again. That was my immediate reaction, distrust of those that I thought had abandoned me, but the more I tried to understand what I had just encountered, the more I decided that it really had to be just a very long, drawn-out dream. Or perhaps I'd just helped out a parallel universe by exposing the horrific behaviour I had filmed on Bradley's phone, which like my new baby, did not return here with me. I really hoped not because I certainly wouldn't have wanted my child left behind in such an evil place.

After what I'd been through, it didn't seem to be much of a stretch to have been trapped in another dimension. It didn't really matter anymore because I was back safe and sound with my friends and family. The hell I had just encountered could be stored away in the depths of my memory and never be released again. Or maybe the whole thing was Emily's fault with her constant complaining about us using self-service and credit cards. That made complete sense. It didn't explain the coma or the supposedly imagined doves that I swear splattered across my windscreen, but the events, possibly.

Somehow all of her rantings had wedged themselves deeply into my subconscious and taken on a life of their own. It all seemed so real, and if labour pains really felt anything like I had just experienced, children were never going to be an option for me. I decided that the only way to move on from what I had obviously not been through was to blame Emily and all the ridiculous horror movies I was now never going to watch again.

My early release from hospital shocked the medical fraternity as I had awoken from a three year sleep with no muscle weakness at all. They couldn't explain my miraculous recovery, but they never understood the reason for my coma-like state to begin with. I wasn't sharing my incredible theory with them because they wouldn't have believed it anymore than I wanted to.

I arrived home to my flat in the exact same mess that I had left it in three years ago. I would have thought they could have cleaned it up for me, but the fridge was filled with at least two weeks of my mother's pre-cooked dinners. It was wonderful to return to the place I once considered beneath me with my beautiful clothes waiting exactly where I left them.

I turned on my larger than necessary television and grabbed my favourite dress from the wardrobe and strangely cuddled it. I was so excited to put it on that I threw the hideous clothes my mother had brought to the hospital straight into the bin. Standing in front of the mirror clothed in a cheap set of underwear, I noticed a strange mark along my stomach. It was a barely healed slash that looked awfully like a wound caused by a sharp tree branch. I must have somehow injured myself while I was asleep, or the hospital staff were doing evil things to me in my corpse-like state.

On closer investigation I noticed very light scars over my arms and face. They were a little more obvious on my forehead. It didn't matter as I decided that the hospital's mistreatment of me had obviously caused me to dream up the whole barbed wire, running-through-the-bushes incident and possibly pushed on my stomach causing the feelings of labour pains.

I was never going to question it, as I didn't need answers for dismissing what I'd been through to be debunked. I was home, I was alive and I was happy, and no stupid little scars were going to ruin that. I was however going to deal with my questionable behaviour that I felt helped to cause the accident I obviously deserved.

Although a little foggy I remembered mistreating an elderly gentleman for not accepting my card. I resolved to return to that store to apologise to that poor man that I had treated so badly. At least I could gain something from my imaginary experience.

I went down to my car that had been fixed and cleaned. There was the twenty dollar note still sitting in plain sight on the console. I needed to return to the shop where I had previously thrown a tantrum and begin changing my ways to prove that I didn't deserve the horrendous fate I had suffered in my supposed coma.

I loaded my wonderful CD player after leaning forward to give it an appreciative kiss. I didn't notice any changes along the road. It was as if I had never left, until I came across the now-missing block of shops. That quaint little block had now become a giant concrete supermarket, as if it had crashed down from above and swallowed the lot.

My abusive predictions had turned into an ugly reality. All I could hope was that my lovely old shopkeeper might have owned it, a ridiculous idea but handily one I was never going to be able to completely rule out.

I ventured into the giant shop that was completely full of its own branded products. Every item was covered with the identical powder blue store nametag, which looked very uninviting and eerily like a world that I had just come from and that I was trying to wipe from my memory. It was horrific to walk through the lifeless store that I had recently dreamed of, and it was becoming harder to believe that there wasn't some other evil scenario attached to my three years in la-la land.

I had to try to fix something by at least paying for a drink in cash, so I found a can of lukewarm home-brand soda and took it towards the only cashier-manned register. Where had all the popular brands disappeared to? Where were my favourite soda cans and chocolate? Why was my ridiculously long dream sequence now playing out in front of me?

I'd had a three year dream of heaven followed by hell. I'd awoken to what I thought was safety but this place was scaring me back into my nightmare. I'd been given an insight into some hideous future, without learning any way to prevent it from happening. I didn't ask for this responsibility. Whatever greater force caused me to suffer, it had picked the wrong patsy. I was no hero, and I didn't want to be. I was a nobody with no answers or resources to change anything that I had just seen. It made no sense to afford me this responsibility when it was not within my power to change it.

Then I noticed him stacking shelves with the nondescript chocolate bars. It was the elderly shopkeeper I had abused and treated so poorly. It was sad to see him dressed in the badly designed shop uniform. In many ways I hoped that he didn't remember me but I knew that I still needed to apologise for my atrocious behaviour. As I walked towards him, he actually gave me a smile of acknowledgement with a strange sparkle in his eyes.

"Been through a bit since I last saw you," he said.

"I'm really sorry for my behaviour," I replied, hoping that would be the end of that. I didn't want to know how he knew what I'd been through because there was no way he could have. Perhaps he had heard about my accident somehow and felt sorry for me. I just desperately wanted to leave before he spoke further and ruined my excuse for his behaviour, but I was frozen where I stood. There was no escape from his angelic presence.

"You cannot stop the end of humanity you have just witnessed," he continued, saying things that I did not want to hear. Then, in a much sterner voice, he continued, "The two of you must have that child, conceived without the mark."

As I tried desperately to speak and say, what, I'm not sure, the old man disappeared. Mark? How could he know the hell I had just endured, the supposed future ahead? The fact that I had been pregnant? What was he? Some kind of mind-reading freak out to destroy my new-found safety?

I was just going to take this as a symptom of my injuries. I'd been in a coma for three years so it was understandable that I could have been hallucinating. It made perfect sense that my mind had become such a great mush it was able to bring my fears to life in the form of mystical but completely unreal characters.

That explanation didn't ease my fear. Now I was really scared, with the note shaking in one hand and the soft drink becoming flat in the other. The cashier's first words made me wish I had used the self-service.

"Do you know Mr Banks?" she asked, "I saw you talking to him. He's such a lovely man." I did not answer her as I wanted to believe I had just imagined that conversation.

In a mildly terrified state, I handed over my twenty dollar note to her, then she shook her head in surprise and quite rudely let me know that they didn't accept cash in this particular store. I wasn't embarrassed, just mortified that my dream was now becoming a truth that I could not relive.

What I'd seen could have no reality behind it and, even if there was, I couldn't stop it. There was nothing I could do to prevent the world's demise, no matter how many times it reminded me of where I'd been. I wasn't turning to religion or truly believing anything that I had encountered. I had learnt nothing of any use to help, so there was no point in prolonging my torture. I wanted so bad to wipe it all from my memory. I needed it gone, not validated. So I reneged on my purchase, leaving the can on the counter with every intention of just running back to my apartment and locking myself away forever.

Then an eerily familiar voice from behind offered the cashier his card to cover my drink. I reluctantly turned to see that it was the gorgeous guy who had come to my rescue when I'd head-butted my rear-vision mirror. I now remembered it all so clearly. The unattainable man of my dreams, my Mr Perfect, but so much more chilling was the fact that it was Michael.

ABOUT THE AUTHOR

Kate Hansen was born, bred and still lives on Victoria's beautiful Mornington Peninsula.

She has travelled extensively with her husband and son and is also the author of the children's book Bandah.

www.ingramcontent.com/pod-product-compliance
Lightning Source LLC
Chambersburg PA
CBHW060330260626
47160CB00007B/2747